And So Is the Bus

JERUSALEM STORIES

And So Is the Bus

JERUSALEM STORIES

Yossel Birstein

Translated from the Hebrew by
Margaret Birstein, Hana Inbar, and
Robert Manaster

DRYAD PRESS WASHINGTON, D.C.

And So Is the Bus: Jerusalem Stories
Copyright © 2015 Margaret Birstein.
All rights reserved.
Printed in the United States.

The stories in *And So Is the Bus: Jerusalem Stories* are from two
collections published in Israel, *Sipurim rokddim bi-rehovot Yerushalayim*, 2000 (*Stories Dancing in the Streets in Jerusalem*) and *Sipurim
me-ezor ha-shalyah*, 2004 (*Stories from the Realm of Tranquility*).

Book and cover design by Sandy Rodgers
Cover Art by Nurit Shany

Library of Congress Cataloging-in-Publication Data

Birstein, Yossel, author.
  [Sipurim rokdim bi-rehovot Yerushalayim. English]
  And so is the bus : Jerusalem stories / Yossel Birstein ; translated
  from the Hebrew by Margaret Birstein, Hana Inbar, and Robert
  Manaster. -- First English translation.
    pages cm
  Includes bibliographical references.
  ISBN 978-1-928755-23-4
  I. Birstein, Margaret, translator. II. Inbar, Hana, translator. III.
  Manaster, Robert, translator. IV. Title.
  PJ5054.B537S5713 2015
  892.43'6--dc23
                              2015035095

DRYAD PRESS
P.O. Box 11233
Takoma Park, Maryland 20913
www.dryadpress.com

Contents

Foreword

I first entered Israeli artist Yosl Bergner's studio — which does bear some resemblance to Santa's Grotto — on Christmas Eve 1978 and departed with two gifts: a print of his painting "The Butterfly Eaters," for reproduction on a book jacket, and a packet of Yossel Birstein's stories, rendered into English (as ever) by his wife, Margaret. I must have presented the manuscript to my own publishers, because in a letter dated 20 January 1979, Yosl thanks me for passing on Yossel's stories, adding, "Let's hope something will happen with them." Alas, nothing did, at least not in England, though I was able to print a few of them in the mid-1980s, during my tenure as the literary editor of London's *Jewish Chronicle*. I had no part in initiating the present volume, but adding this foreword allows me to feel — however undeservedly — mission accomplished.

It took but a few more visits to Israel — during which I

got to spend time with both Yosl and Yossel (they opted for different transliterations to avoid being confused with each other) — to recognize that they were in fact two parts of a whole; Yosl being the id, and Yossel the ego. This did not mean that one was garrulous and the other timid. On the contrary, if there were still a gold medal for oratory in the Olympics they would have been deadly rivals. No, it was more that Yosl embraced the life of an artist, whereas Yossel was certainly a writer, but also (in chronological order) a shepherd, a bank manager, and an archivist. He was, in fact, the cataloguer of the three-ton archive of Yiddish poet Melech Ravitch — Yosl's father — bequeathed to the National Library in Jerusalem. He showed it to me once; stack after stack, all filled with boxes, like a gigantic shoe-store. Each box contained a life or more, and Yossel knew them all, and a hundred stories about each of them. He was a raconteur of genius, an alchemist with a tongue that could raise the dead. And one by one they returned from the other side, those dreamers of a vanished world.

In the 1930s, sensing the impending catastrophe, Melech Ravitch travelled the globe in search of a refuge for European Jewry. In the end he settled for Australia, and sent for his own family for starters. It was on the boat from Europe that young Bergner and Birstein — born within three weeks of each other in the fall of 1920 — began their lifelong brotherhood. Yossel was sailing to join his grandparents in Australia; the Nazis murdered the remainder of his family, who remained in Biala Podlaska. Yosl responded to the genocide in paint, Yossel in poetry. Ravitch, as recounted elsewhere, judged the poems harshly, and declared them to be without merit. God forbid I should contradict him, but to my mind they are worthy of consideration, because — among other reasons — they expose the pain that is tucked away in Yossel's later prose like some primal wound. The poems are raw lamentations, elegies for a lost brother, a lost sister, a lost father, and a lost mother. In one he pictures his sister, concealed in a neighbor's barn, writing a last letter to her brother in Australia, then imagines the light searching for her shape in the empty space she once inhabited. "It was poetry I chose," he wrote in the collection *Under Alien Skies*, "for neighbor to my grief."

Who can doubt that Ravitch's dismissal prompted misgivings in the latent poet, but I'd hazard that an equally potent catalyst for change was the actual presence of new neighbors. These neighbors were, of course, Israelis. Yossel made Aliyah before Yosl, and was waiting for him in Haifa when he eventually disembarked in 1950. "Behold," he said, "the new Jew." Despite the novelty of the scene he uttered the words not in Hebrew but in Yiddish. It was a language he never abandoned, though he embraced Hebrew too, and the new direction it represented.

When he finally settled in Jerusalem he found himself in a repository of stories — each individual a walking drama. Nabokov strode the mountain slopes of Switzerland, net in hand, in search of butterflies. For Yossel — a less showy writer — the buses of Jerusalem were his Alps, teeming with life and untold stories to collect. His findings were not pinned down to reside moribund in a drawer, but were recreated in succinct prose and released into the world. Out of the most modest of ingredients — Yossel lists one recipe in "How a Story Gets Cooking" — come distillations worthy of Chekhov. It is important to emphasize this life-affirming aspect of his craft, because I have a suspicion that Death was a constant if unspoken stowaway in the buses Yossel rode, like some miserable ticket inspector, and that every one of his brilliant miniatures was a snatched victory for life. Bear in mind that the starting point for many of these voyagings was Kiryat HaYovel, but a stop or two from Yad Vashem. Sure enough one day the Angel of Death caught Yossel off guard and carried him away. But the rest is hardly silence, not when Yossel chooses to sit beside you on Bus 16.

Clive Sinclair
London, England

A Couple of Dots and Lines about Yossel Birstein

Yossel began his literary career as a poet, writing Yiddish poems in Australia. He was eighteen at the time and didn't know any other Yiddish poet who could comment on his poetry and instruct him. But he did have one good friend — Yosl Bergner, who later became one of Israel's most renowned painters. Both Yossel and Yosl made their journey from Poland to Australia together and became lifelong best friends. At the time Yossel Birstein was making his first steps in poetry, Yosl Bergner was already a full-fledged painter, with quite a few artists among his acquaintances. But most important of all — he himself was the son of Melech Ravitch, the most renowned Yiddish poet of the time.

As a favor to his son, Melech Ravitch agreed to take a look at Yossel Birstein's poems. Some very long weeks passed by before Yosl Bergner was able to come back with his father's verdict.

"Raise up your thumb," he instructed Birstein. He did.

"Now cover the fingernail with your other thumb." He did that too.

"A bit more," instructed Bergner, and Birstein complied.

"Now, what do you see?" Bergner asked.

"The tip of the tip of my fingernail," replied Birstein.

"That," said Yosl Bergner, "according to my father, Melech Ravitch, is how big your talent is: a tip of a tip of a fingernail!"

So Yossel switched from poetry to prose.

Yossel was born in a shtetl called Biala Podlaska in the northeastern part of Poland. He spent the first sixteen years of his life in this shtetl, which was almost exclusively a Yiddish-speaking environment.

In 1936 his parents sent him to Australia to join his grandparents who were already living there. That was the last time Yossel saw his parents. Four years later, they, along with almost everyone else who spoke Yiddish, passed away from this world in the Holocaust.

The next fourteen years of Yossel's life were spent in Australia, an English-speaking environment. A long enough time for him to fall in love, get married, have a child (me), and adopt English as the spoken language between him and his wife (my mother) for the rest of their lives. But not enough time for English to replace Yiddish, his *boich loshen*, a term he coined, which literally means "stomach language."

Yossel was already thirty when he and his little family made Aliyah, and the remaining fifty-three years of his life were spent in a Hebrew speaking environment: a dozen years in Kibbutz Gevat, where his second daughter, Nurit, was born, another dozen in Kiryat Tivon, yet another dozen in Upper Nazareth, and all the rest in Jerusalem. Fifty-three years is, no doubt, a lifetime, but when a new language enters your life at the age of thirty, it never becomes your gut language.

So here was an avid storyteller, walking around in the world without a native language to tell his stories in. What do you do? You tell stories without a language. You wage war against words. You use as few of them as possible. You need to be able to use them like the brush at the hands of Picasso: an eye, a hand, a nipple — a woman!

And where is the best place to learn how to do it? The

local city buses in Jerusalem. A big city, many bus lines, many bus stops, and a very short distance between one stop and the next. A person who entered your life at one stop might leave it for good at the very next one. But the urge to tell you his or her story is sometimes generations long. So there, on the bus, people find ways of telling their lifelong stories in just a few words.

A short time after Yossel moved to Jerusalem, he began publishing a weekly story in *Kol Ha'Ir* (*The Voice of the City*). These stories became very popular, and for many years, he met people on and off the buses who were "dancing in the streets of Jerusalem." Yossel also "invited" long-dead relatives and neighbors from his childhood shtetl, as well as acquaintances from his years in Australia, for short bus rides — they fit right in!

In 2000, *Stories Dancing in the Streets of Jerusalem* was published and it's from this book that we have selected most of the stories for *And So Is the Bus*.

A professor of Japanese culture once compared Birstein's stories to those of the Japanese writer Yasunari Kawabata, known for his "Palm of the Hand Stories" — short stories that can fit into the palm of the hand. Throughout the years, however, Yossel perfected his art to the point of actually writing "fingernail stories." Many of them were collected in his book *A Patch of Silence*. Towards the end of his life, when he was already too ill to sit up and write, he used to dictate them to me. Every morning, as I entered my office, I received over the phone a complete story of just a few sentences. A story left for him, he used to say, under the pillow, by the Angel of Dreams.

After he passed, these stories were published in the final collection *Stories from the Realm of Tranquility*. Some of them are, to my mind, superb "tip of the tip of the fingernail" stories, giving Melech Ravitch's early verdict of Yossel's talent a very ironic twist. Here is one of them:

> I've finished my reserves duty in the army and was walking back home along a path in a deep canyon.
>
> On both sides of the path, soldiers were still training. One of them waved out to me, came down to the path and asked me where I was going.
>
> "I've finished my reserves duty and I'm going back home," I told him.
>
> "On this path?" He asked.
>
> "I came on this path," I explained, "and surely this is the path that leads back home."

"You've finished your reserves duty in the army," he said, "and you don't know that this path doesn't lead you home?"

I looked around and said, "But there aren't any other paths here, this is the only one."

He too looked around and said, "Right. There aren't any other paths."

Hana Inbar
Kefar Sava, Israel

And So Is the Bus

JERUSALEM STORIES

Blood Connection

WHEN YOCHANAN ZAID[1] CAME TO VISIT ME FROM the North, I hosted him on a city bus in Jerusalem. We boarded Bus 1 on Prophet Deborah Street, at the stop near the Ministry of Education whose many windows were glancing cross-eyed at the Ungarin houses and also at the neighborhood churches. Let's go back and forth, exchange a word or two on the many years we haven't seen one another, and perhaps I'd find out about the family connection he had with an Arab woman.

The woman had appeared in his backyard one summer evening when Yochanan was hosting me there. She asked him to put in a good word for her son who was in prison.

Yochanan thought she was mistaken. It wasn't him but me she should've turned to. I was sitting next to him and we were having a cold drink. He pointed at me and noted each of my occupations: a do-gooder, a writer, an active member on the Committee for Human Rights.

In those days Yochanan and I were neighbors in Kiryat Tivon, and we were living in the Zaid neighborhood, named after his father, Alexander Zaid, who was murdered in his prime by an Arab. After his death, as appropriate for an Israeli hero, a founder of Hashomer Ha-Ivri,[2] a bronze monument of him on the horse he was riding over the fields of Galilee and Valley of Jezreel was erected on top of the hill, galloping skyward. Yochanan's house stood at the foot of this hill.

The woman shook her head and said she wasn't mistaken. She didn't know any Jew but him, and she came especially for him. He should go with her to the prison and put in a good word for her son, who wasn't in politics and wasn't a thief.

Yochanan shook his head too. He had never met the woman. She seemed to him quite normal. Poised, tall, wearing sunglasses. Her long dress and headscarf were colorful: flowers, birds flying. But what did all this have to do with him?

"Family connection," answered the woman and pointed at the statue in the shadow of which we were sitting.

Yochanan stood up to shake off her words. He was a Jew, she an Arab. And they had a family connection? What else could she possibly tell him? He emptied his cup in one gulp and without waiting for an answer disappeared into his house.

The woman remained standing. Her feet were bare. Yochanan did not hurry back. Something similar happened to me with him when we first became neighbors. I told him one day, not without pride, that as a young man in Melbourne, Australia, I had read a Yiddish poem in praise of his father, Alexander Zaid, who gave his life in God's name for the Freedom of the Land. I mentioned the poet's name, H. Leivick, and quoted two lines from the poem. Then too Yochanan jumped up from his seat, disappeared into the house, and returned after a long while, putting a condition on our friendship: that I should never ever mention his father to him again.

He was no longer young, had a family of his own, but the anger of a child deprived of his father was still burning in him. Anger at his father's killers, anger at those who praised his deeds. He hadn't forgiven either of them. He had already sacrificed enough as a ten-year-old, and was now exempt from lifting a finger to help others.

Since then I was careful not to mention his father to him, and we went on sitting from time to time in the shadow of the statue, exchanging a word or two to break the long silences.

Now too, on the bus making its way to the Wailing Wall, our silence continued along streets bustling with people. At the intersection of Tribes of Israel and Jaffa the bus stopped at the red light. We exchanged glances and followed some passersby crossing the street. Three Chasidim with shtreimels and kapotas, three nuns with habits and crosses, all crowded in black. For a moment they looked like one family.

Yochanan let out a coughing smile. The cough — from smoking and old age, the smile — at the sight of the family of Chasidim and nuns, and at the billboard on the wall behind them.

The billboard called on the residents of the Ungarin houses to all come out and watch a movie about saying Selichot in the city of Kiev, Ukraine.[3] Men alone and women alone, on separate days. In big bright letters the billboard promised an exciting experience for the whole family.

Unable to hold back, I reminded Yochanan of his family connection. When he had returned to the yard, he offered a glass of water to the Arab woman so she'd drink and go, and never repeat this nonsense of hers. A family connection, indeed. The woman refused the drink, and said that their connection was even stronger. It was a blood connection.

Yochanan stood facing her, repeating her words with scorn, and the woman nodded her head, insisting she was telling the truth.

"And what is this blood connection between us?" asked Yochanan.

She wouldn't answer him in my presence. She'd tell him in the house, face to face.

Yochanan asked me to wait a minute. The woman must be crazy. He would see her out of his house through the front door.

A short while afterward Yochanan came back and asked me to go home. We would carry on another time. He was taking the woman in his car to the nearby prison and would have a word with whomever he needed to. They knew him there and who his father had been, and perhaps he'd be able to have her son released on bail. She was right, he added, there was a blood connection between them.

When the bus stopped near the Jaffa Gate of the Old City, we took a short walk and managed to return on the very same bus to the central station. There, Yochanan boarded the bus to Haifa, and from Haifa, he told me, he would take a taxi back to Zaid Hill. He was pleased with the visit to Jerusalem, and was amazed that I still remembered in detail his encounter with the Arab woman. Now he was also willing to tell me what she had told him face to face.

It was her father who killed his father.

A Wet Man by the Traffic Light

AFTERWARD THE WOMAN GREW SILENT. EARLIER THAT gray morning, she negotiated between the bus driver and the man who stood outside wet from the rain, banging his fist on the closed door. She was sitting next to me in the front seat, and called the driver by name:

"Moshe!"

The driver, his eyes fixed on the rows of cars stretching all the way to the red light, turned his head slowly toward the door and asked:

"What does he want, the idiot?"

"He's my neighbor," she softly answered. Her hands were busy holding baskets on her knees and she pointed at him with her elbow: a bearded man with a black hat wrapped in a transparent plastic bag.

"He wants to get in," she said.

The distant red light turned green. Cars at the front of the two rows began moving lazily. Here and there honks were heard, and the rain turned to hail. The wet man kept banging on the sealed door. At his back the wind lifted the tallit tossed over his shoulders. The woman freed her hand momentarily, and with two fingers touched her temple.

"Lost his mind," she said.

The driver increased the wiper speed and started driving slowly. The other side of the road was empty of people and cars. Through the haze you could make out the wall surrounding the military section of the Mount of Rest at Herzl Boulevard.[1] The woman shifted her fingers from her head to the wall:

"That's where his lost mind is buried."

The wet man was running along the locked door without banging on it. When the bus left him behind, his tallit spread out into a flapping wing, and the transparent pinkish bag filled up with air. The woman bent her two fingers one by one, calling out the names of his two sons, Hillel and David, whom he lost in two different wars.

"They lie together, grave by grave," she said. He himself,

she went on, was one of the first residents in the neighbor-hood. On Saturday mornings he used to sit on the low wall by the bridge, cracking sunflower seeds and scattering bless-ings. He didn't change his habit when his first son fell. He kept cracking seeds and scattering blessings even when his second son fell. His third son died in a car accident. He wanted to have him buried next to his two brothers in the military section, but they didn't permit him. That's when he started losing his mind. Stopped cracking seeds and scatter-ing blessings. He grew a beard, put on a black hat, wrapped himself in a tallit, and day by day, in rain or shine, went to pray at the two separate mountains, the Mount of Rest at Herzl Boulevard and the Mount of Rest at Givat Shaul.

"Poor man. Always in a hurry," said the woman, and again caught hold of the big basket that jolted on her knees when the bus suddenly stopped, this time in the middle of the intersection in front of the red light. The driver didn't make it through the yellow, and the bus bit into the striped crossing. He leaned his elbows on the wheel and his hands supported his bent head. Hail started banging on the bus's roof, and before the light changed, the wet man reappeared at the closed door.

"Moshe!" called the woman.

The driver raised an elbow, and through the triangle his arm made he threw a glance at the door and hissed:

"What does he want, the idiot?"

The Crumb Picker

THE THIN MAN WITH THE THICK BEARD DIDN'T WASTE even a second when he sat down next to me on Bus 15. He opened the bag he placed on his knees and drew out a large piece of cheesecake, side-glancing at me to make sure I was looking away. You could see he needed it. Apart from the bulky bag and the black beard there was nothing about him he could be proud of. The blessing he mumbled and the first bite of cake were swallowed in an instant, without any space between them. The whole slice nearly gone, his beard was sown with crumbs.

I wasn't looking away. I pressed my face to the window to look at the outside. Line 15 had a long way to go, starting at the Katamon neighborhood and finishing at Givat Shaul. The outside between neighborhoods wasn't standing still. It was changing colors several times, and the human landscape wasn't staying far behind: flowery clothes, black garments. The names of the streets were awe inspiring: HaPalmach.[1] Ze'ev Jabotinsky.[2] Kings of Israel. And there were buildings of grandeur: Jerusalem Theater. Islamic Museum.[3] Presidential Residence.

In the meantime the man finished his cake and was diligently picking the crumbs out of his beard, tossing them one by one into his mouth. He did that gracefully, gently. I couldn't resist the temptation. I gave up the Theater and President, and turned my attention to the crumbs. Within a moment I was all his. He turned to me and asked:

"Sir, do you have diabetes?" His voice was very pleasant. He could be proud of it too.

"No," I answered.

He dug into the open bag, and I was afraid he was going to draw out another large piece of cake and offer it to me, and I wouldn't be able to resist. But he drew out a pinkish sheet, presented it to me, and said that if I read what's written there, I would never ever have diabetes. I sighed with relief and reached for the paper. With his free hand the man caught another crumb and said it was for a price:

"Three shekels."

We made a deal. I took the paper, he took the money, then added:

"You need to read it to the end."

"I'll read it at home," I said. His beard, his voice, his bag — all conveyed authority. I rolled the paper into a tube, and while I was stuffing it into my pocket, he turned to me again and asked:

"Sir, do you have high blood pressure?"

"No," I answered.

Meanwhile, the bus already passed Jaffa and Strauss streets. It stopped at Shabbat Square, waiting amid the never-ending rush. A yellow joined red on the traffic light, and an ambulance's wail burst onto the scene. It blared by us, wiggling between cars, wigs, black hats, though it didn't silence my neighbor's voice. This time he drew out a grayish sheet from a different section in his bulky bag. If I read what's written there, he said, I would never ever have high blood pressure.

"Three shekels," he announced.

We made another deal. I took the paper, he took the money and ordered me to read it to the end.

"I'll read it at home," I answered, and stuffed the grayish paper as a tube into my pocket.

The ambulance sounded faraway, but the rush on Kings of Israel Street did not stop. A Chasid with a white yarmulke cut in front of our bus. He had hunched shoulders like my rabbi in Poland. When telling us toddlers about Jerusalem, our rabbi probably had this neighborhood in mind, where the prophets owned the streets, and prayers and business deals were floating in the air, not resting for a moment. My neighbor, the healer, noticed I was following the commotion in the street, and even guessed my thoughts when he turned to me and asked:

"Sir, and about the liberation of Jerusalem did you hear?"

"No."

I drew from my pocket three more shekels and held them out, not without fear that the liberation of Jerusalem would probably cost a lot more than high blood pressure. But he ignored the money, drew out from his bag a blank sheet and said that he hadn't yet written the story. He didn't have its ending. Once he knew the end, he'd put the liberation of Jerusalem in writing. In the meantime I'd have to wait.

"Wait until when?" I asked, and noticed the last white crumb hidden deep in the thickness of his black beard.

He knew what he was talking about. Without an ending there's no story. I was wondering whether he would find them, the missing end and the last crumb in his beard. They both made noise in my head.

Gently the man returned the empty sheet to its place, and I, wishing to silence the noise in my head, rose a little from my seat. Still willing to make a deal, I asked again, my voice all prayer:

"Sir, wait until when?"

When the man saw me rising, he too got up and pressed the stop button. While we were standing face to face, a lady who was sitting behind me tapped my shoulder, called me by name, and asked in a whisper if I already had a new Jerusalem story. Before I was able to turn around and see her face, the man caught her whisper and asked:

"From Jerusalem?"

"Yes."

"How many generations?"

"A dozen years," I answered softly.

The man spread out his fingers into his beard, captured

the last crumb, tossed it into his mouth and turned away from me. I put the shekels back into my pocket, and turned to the young lady, her shy smile hidden in the corners of her mouth. Not yet, I told her, you must wait. Without an end, there's no story.

The Love Dance

FTER THE DEMONSTRATION THAT HADN'T TAKEN place, I bumped into both of them — the young Chasid and the female reporter. I was walking behind the reporter on the narrow sidewalk of Mea Shearim Street, and her blonde, uncombed ponytail swayed before my eyes. The Chasid burst onto the scene in a white cab, stuck his head out of the window, and yelled an insult from Genesis:

"Hittite!"

Even earlier, at the Shomrei Emunim Square, while I was waiting with the blonde reporter for the demonstration to start, the Chasid yelled another insult from the same book. Some kind of compliment, thought the young reporter, since from where she was standing, in the narrow shadow of the lamppost, she waved gracefully with a few fingers toward the man who was standing on a makeshift stage, checking the microphone and loudspeakers scattered here and there on the roofs of the Ungarin houses. His wide-rimmed black hat and white shirt brought out his yellowish sidelocks curling down to his broad shoulders, the sun weaving threads of gold into them.

The Chasid brought the microphone close to his lips and called toward her in a voice that shook the nearby houses:

"Jebusite!"

The young woman, bare-skinned and tan, moved in her long dress hanging down to her thin-heeled sandals, and her ponytail dashed forward snuggling around her long thin neck.

She came to cover the event for her newspaper, she told me. Apart from us no one had yet arrived to protest the desecration of ancient bones.[1] The heat grew heavier in the afternoon hours.

"Hirsch-Zalman! Where are the posters?" shouted the Chasid from the platform toward a tall thin guy with a scanty beard and a raised right shoulder, who appeared at the other side of the square near the small market stalls. Hirsch-Zalman raised his crooked shoulder even higher, answered he was too hot to carry the posters, and hid himself in the shadow of one of the empty market stalls.

Some kids gathered around the platform, and one of them, frail with glasses, pointed at the reporter, calling her "the naked female," and asked the Chasid if they could start throwing stones at her.

The reporter came out from the narrow shadow of the lamppost, sent an embarrassed smile toward the man on the platform, and turned to go away from the place. She told me she wouldn't go back to her newspaper empty-handed, and so would walk around the neighborhood. The Chasid was annoyed that no posters were brought over, no minyan of Jews gathered for Mincha, the afternoon prayer, and no one had turned up to chant psalms from the stage. Angrily he took apart the microphone stand and disappeared into a nearby building.

He turned up again as I was walking behind the young woman, his head sticking out from an open window of the white cab. Even after his second call from the cab, he wouldn't let go of her. He told the cab driver to slow down. They moved on together: she on the narrow sidewalk, he pushing his head out of the cab's window. He yelled at her a third time:

"Perizzite!"

She didn't turn her head. She continued on her way. Only her ponytail increased its swing across the narrow sidewalk. For a moment she disappeared from the Chasid's sight behind a black pickup parked with its two right wheels on the sidewalk. When she reappeared, the white cab had already stopped. The Chasid jumped out leaving the door wide open behind him, and stood in front of her in all his grandeur, with the tallit katan as armor across his ironed shirt.

"Slut!" he shouted to her face.

She stopped in her tracks, stuck. Her ponytail didn't move. But she didn't let him take charge, she paid him back in the same tongue:

"You pious shmuck!"

The Chasid grabbed the blonde ponytail and pulled until her head got nearly plucked back. The reporter grabbed the golden sidelocks and pulled too. Her upper body arched backward, and because of her pull the Chasid nearly bent over her. Both looked as if in the midst of a love dance.

Another young Chasid, a redhead in black with a white yarmulke, stepped in. He tore them apart, and while doing so, the reporter's sunglasses fell off and her eyes reflected panic. More young Chasidim surrounded her, and the red-head in black raised a stick over her head.

She retreated to the wall, and with both hands flipped up her long dress. Let them take a look and freak out.

"Scat!" she shouted at the young Chasid.

Sharply, she bent down and stepped out of her sandals. Spotting the open door of the white cab, she disappeared into it. The Chasid shoved his long sidelocks under his black hat and searched around with a murderous look. Not seeing the girl, he too dashed into the cab and slammed the door behind him. The cab set out on its way with angry honks. The corner threads of the Chasid's tallit-katan, caught by the closed door, were flapping in the warm wind. Just before the cab disappeared, its door opened and closed and the threads were gathered in.

The people dispersed. A passing bus crushed the discarded sunglasses. On the narrow sidewalk, close to the wall, a pair of sandals remained, poised on heels high and thin.

Something Good in This Country

THE MAN SITTING BEHIND THE DRIVER WINKED AT ME to sit next to him when I got on the last bus before Shabbat. He moved his green basket aside and also his prosthetic leg. Tapping it lightly, he said: "From Russia."

When the bus moved on, he added: "Fine wood. Twenty-two years in Israel, the wood didn't go bad. It didn't dry in the sun and even worms couldn't get the better of it. There's nothing like it. Go ahead, try and find one other good thing in this country of ours."

The upper part of his wooden leg reflected in the mirror above the driver's head. The pant leg was rolled up above his knee. I nodded in agreement and would have kept nodding, but at the next stop he gestured for me to stop. He caught sight of a young woman who got on the bus. When she passed us by, he pointed at her red pants and said someone like that, unfortunately, would no doubt prefer a whole man. He learned it firsthand when his wife passed away here in Jerusalem, in the Neve Yaakov neighborhood. Had he been a whole man, some girl in red or another color would have knocked on his door and brought him a hot meal. But half men, he found out, don't make a career in the Jewish State. So, he was forced to cook his own miserable meals and had upset his stomach.

He asked me to hold his green basket for a moment, and wipe that look of pity off my face. No pity please. He was not a man to make an issue of it. He didn't make an issue when he lost his leg in the Red Army, somewhere on the way from Moscow to Berlin. He didn't make tzimmes over[1] his wife's death, and he wasn't making tzimmes over his diarrhea.

Again I nodded, and gestured that's what happens to a lonely man in this world of ours. I felt sorry that on our short ride along Jaffa Street, and later along Herzl Boulevard, I wasn't able to find anything else we could both agree on and say, "It was good." Even his wooden leg, which at the beginning was good, lost its glamour along the ride.

He sat next to me and urged the driver to hurry, since he was pressed for time. Shabbbat was approaching and he needed to hitchhike to Ein Karem, or if no choice, get there by foot, carrying a heavy basket.

"What's in the basket?" I asked.

There were all sorts of good things in it. Toys and sweets, a cake and bottles of wine; all of these for his grandkids, for his two sons and their wives, and for his daughter and her husband — all married!

"A family gathering," he said, and pressed the stop button as the bus crossed the Ein Karem intersection, approaching the street across from the huge, red, iron sculpture.[2]

I handed him the green basket and helped him get off the bus. At the last moment, when he was already standing on the sidewalk, I called toward him excitedly that I did find something else good in the Jewish State:

"Family!" I called out. "Your family!"

The man lifted his basket and started stepping toward the tall arches of the sculpture — gates open to all directions — then turned to me and called toward the bus: "Family? My family? Get as far away from them as possible!"

Customer on the Way

IN THE END I DIDN'T TRY ON THE SHOES. BECAUSE THE man died.

About a month earlier, while he sat next to me on Bus 11 on its way to the Mount of Rest in Givat Shaul, he took an interest in my shoes. He wanted to know if I felt comfortable in them. When he heard I'd been comfortable in them for the past twenty years, he said he had a similar pair in his shoe shop on Jaffa Street, made by the same factory. I should come by and try them on.

Less than a week later I was on my way there. I arrived a little late because of a suspicious package. The police stopped traffic in both directions when I was already close to the shop. Between Davidka Square and Mahaneh Yehuda Market, the shop owner had said, and added I'd recognize the shop easily. Dust in the window.

On the bus he looked dressed for a special occasion. A Shabbat suit, colorful tie, white yarmulke, a flower pinned to his lapel. He was on his way to visit his dead. Son. Daughter. Wife. Once a month he brought them news from the street and from the shop. From the shop there wasn't any news, no customers either. This time he'd tell them about me. Not every day does one meet a person comfortable in the same pair of shoes for twenty years. When he found out I lived many years in Australia, he wanted to know if there too, in that faraway continent, one praised an object by saying it was like an old shoe.

His neighbors, the nearby shop owners, would make fun of him, calling his shop *Alteh Zachn*.[1] The owner on the right outdid them all — glasscutter, ill tempered, and a Kohen.[2] This one refused to enter the shop, claiming the shoeboxes on the shelves reminded him of a cemetery. A Kohen is not allowed to approach the dead.

He pinned the flower deeper into his lapel, and wondered that I hadn't asked him why he wasn't selling modern shoes rather than old ones like mine. Before I had a chance to ask he already answered. He didn't understand the crazy rush for machine-made shoes. Before he became a shoe merchant he was a shoemaker. A shoe that hadn't passed through a shoemaker's hand, he knew it wasn't real.

The suspicious package was removed. The traffic opened but the shop was already closed. The glasscutter was standing outside, nervously biting the edge of his thin beard.

"Gone," he told me and pointed at the sign above the dusty shop window. In faded letters, the sign said: "Shoes for Eternity — Ezekiel Yish-Tamim."[3] Pairs of shoes like mine were lying on shelves in the shop window. Shoes without laces, of the kind that slipped on a foot without effort, as Ezekiel Yish-Tamim pointed out on the bus when he asked me to lift up one foot so that he could check its sole. Even before I did, he was ready to swear the little nails holding it were wooden, not iron. Why? This too he was going to tell his dead, the son who was murdered in India, the daughter who ended her own life, the wife who died of a broken heart. On winter days when you step into puddles, he told me while I was lifting my foot, the sole expands, the holes expand with it, and iron nails pop out. Wooden nails not so. They expand along with the holes and hold on to the sole. I may, he said, take his words as a parable for his own life. He himself was a wooden nail. One of these days his neighbors, the shop-keepers on Jaffa Street, were going to be surprised at the long line stretching in front of his shop. They would stand outside and look on with awe at the winding line, people of all ages pushing to enter and try on shoes.

I came upon the long line a month later when I was on my way to his shop a second time. From some distance it looked as if another suspicious package was found. But the traffic flowed in both directions. By the shop, however, two policemen were keeping order. The shelves in the shop were already empty. A large obituary notice was posted on the window, on behalf of the Soldiers Relief Organization, mourning the passing of the donor Ezekiel Yish-Tamim. The ill-tempered glasscutter was standing outside, still biting the edge of his beard, and urging a modestly dressed girl to join the line and buy herself shoes at half price. He died suddenly, he told her, and left all his possessions to the soldiers. House, shop, everything. No wonder they called the police. It's already the third day and there's no end to the shoes. People gather outside the shop hours before it opens. He himself was among the first. The glasscutter lifted a foot to show the girl. I too looked. A pair of shoes like mine, without laces. The same ones I saw in the window a month ago, but no longer dusty.

"Shoes for eternity," added the glasscutter.

"Ezekiel Yish-Tamim," I said to myself. On the bus I didn't know his name and he didn't know mine. He shook my hand when we parted at Givat Shaul Cemetery. He shook it strongly, bent slightly forward, and the flower fell out of his lapel. He picked it up, put it back in place, and stepped forward to meet his dead.

Herzl Boulevard on a Rainy Day

THIS STORY IS ABOUT TWO DROPS OF WATER ON A RAINY day in mid-winter, on Bus 20, but a question comes before it:

How does Shabbat first enter Jerusalem?
And the answer:
On the last city bus.

The driver is bald, and I, the only passenger, am sitting behind him in the front seat. The empty space behind us, with all its empty seats, is full of Shabbat.

My bald head is reflecting in the mirror above the driver. He stops at a red light on Herzl Boulevard. On the right, the wall of the Mount of Rest; on the left, a police car blinking a blue light. It's raining. Through the front window the view is threatening. Lightning has already sliced the gray. Thunder, taking its time, is sure to come. Wipers are moving without catching a breath. Rain is pounding on the bus roof. A man's fist is pounding on the closed door. A man with a beard and a wide-brimmed black hat.

My eyes meet the driver's in the mirror above him and the two bald heads look very much alike, in complete agreement about the man outside. He will not enter. The door will not open for him.

The thunder came and went. The rain continued to pour. The gray continued to threaten. Even the blue light on the police car blinked threats. That's all the driver needs: to be fined in honor of Shabbat for opening the door at a red light in front of the police.

This scene popped up in my head like magic, in mid-summer, when I got on Bus 20 with the same driver. I held out my monthly pass. He cast a quick glance at me and repeated the same movement from that rainy Shabbat evening, but this time as a dry run. With his palm he wiped the full width of his bald head from ear to ear.

I sat in the first seat behind him, wishing to have a word, or at least meet his eyes in the mirror above. I wanted to ask what happened there, in that moment of rain: red light in front, cemetery on the right, police on the left, and the wet man at the door that wouldn't open.

The door did open and the man got in. Outside he looked small, but inside he was very tall. His hat nearly touched the ceiling. A part of its front rim tilted down. He held out his ticket to be punched, and when the driver reached down for the ticket puncher, the man bent forward over him and said:

"Sir, thank you very much for opening the door for me," and a swollen raindrop gathered at the tilted rim and landed on the driver's bald head.

The driver returned the punched ticket and gestured for him to enter further into his parlor. He looked at the red light. The swollen raindrop reflecting in the mirror slid toward his right ear.

Now too, in mid-summer, I wasn't able to have a word with him. Not even our eyes met in the mirror above him. The bus was filling up with passengers. The road was filling up with cars.

The wet passenger followed the driver's request and took five steps into the depth of Shabbat space. Suddenly he stopped, as if in front of another door that wouldn't open.

He turned and walked back. While the driver was bending down to put the ticket puncher in its place, the man with the wide hat lowered his head and said:

"Sir, even if you hadn't opened the door for me, even then I would have thanked you very very much."

A second raindrop gathered on the hat's rim and landed on the driver's bald head, reflecting in the mirror.

The light changed. The bus moved. The police car passed us in a hurry. The wall of the Mount of Rest disappeared behind us, and the second drop started sliding in the opposite direction, toward the driver's left ear.

The Message

I SLAMMED THE DOOR AND WAS OUTSIDE. THE WINDOWS rattled. Let my daughter know I won't be back home soon. First I needed to calm down. A bus ride might help. I'd go to a distant neighborhood, walk a bit, then go back home. And if that didn't help, I'd get on another bus, another neighborhood. Jerusalem's a city of neighborhoods. It's just a pity there was only one man waiting at the nearby stop. I must have missed the bus. I'd have asked the man if he was waiting long. But he was standing at the sidewalk's edge, with his dark glasses and cane in hand, talking to himself. I turned away, faced a wall, and started talking to myself. The trembling windows set off by the door-slam back home kept quivering in my head. What did she want from me, my daughter? With her malicious smile she wanted to know what I'd say if one fine day, she, Nurit, a high school junior, would come home from school and tell me she was pregnant.

"Pregnant by whom?"

No reaction.

She tricked me. To prove that I was blind to her concerns. That I didn't understand her. That she was already old enough to choose her own way in life. That I shouldn't push myself into a world that wasn't mine.

Frightened thoughts like the windows at my house filled my head, and there was no sign of a bus. The man in the dark glasses kept on talking to himself, and no other passengers arrived. Had there been a longer line for the next bus, I would have felt at ease. The day before I found myself standing in a long line, impatiently waiting for a bus that was late. Nagging thoughts were buzzing in my head, depressing ones were digging into my soul. But then, a man who stood behind me lost his temper, and for an instant the nagging thoughts left me and settled on him. It was indeed a very short-lived break, but a worthwhile one. Like that hippopotamus I once saw in the middle of a very hot dry day, his back full of flies and his tail too short. He started plodding toward the pool, entering it at his leisure, and when all covered with water but for a thin layer of back, he dove then came up some distance away. In the meantime a cloud of flies hovered above the water in a frenzied buzz: Where's the back? On the other side of the pool, for a short moment on a very hot dry day, the hippopotamus was standing without the flies.

This time there was no line, and the man in the dark glasses kept on talking to himself. So I talked to my daughter. Nurit, I told her, and stopped. What did I have to tell her apart from angry words. The argument between us had long slid into quarrel. Pregnant?

I asked her if she was able to understand me. If the pregnancy was her own concern, or mine too. If she saw me at all.

"Aren't you yourself blind?" I shouted at her, and repeated the question here at the bus stop as I faced the wall. The more I repeated the question the angrier I got. No sight of the bus. I wish it would get here. Just getting on the bus does something to me. The ticket, the punch-click, the search for a comfortable seat. Passengers all around. Windows. I heard myself shouting in a whisper, where are you, Bus!

Eventually the bus arrived, and I didn't get on. There was no need. I returned home totally calm.

"What happened?" my daughter asked, her voice still sarcastic, her smile still spiteful. "Calmed down so soon?" I heard her asking.

"Go out," I told her, "and don't forget to slam the door. Hard, until the windows tremble. And wait for a bus. It doesn't matter which line. If you're lucky, what happened to me will happen to you, and you too will calm down right then and there. Your beautiful eyes will soften, and you won't be blind anymore."

The man who waited with me at the bus stop wasn't talking to himself. He was talking to me. But in my irritation I failed to read the signs: dark glasses, cane in hand. He raised his voice and asked why I wasn't listening to him. He needed a favor. When the bus arrived, I should help him get on. He wasn't able to tell by sound the difference between an old bus and a new one. The step on the old one was very steep, recently he banged his leg and the wound hadn't healed yet. He asked that I bend down and help lift his leg. I bent down and lifted it. When he was standing with both feet on the step, I felt he was falling out. I held his leg fast with one hand, raised my other to his back and pushed him in. Then I heard a woman's voice calling from inside the bus:

"Why are you pushing? Don't you see a blind woman is getting off?"

Stolen Glance

I DIDN'T FEEL COMFORTABLE SHOWING THE MAN IN A TIE
he annoyed me when he first forced me to sit next to him
on my way to work. Later, when I got used to him, I was
actually glad he took the trouble of saving me the seat. Then
he died without warning and I missed him. Every morning
I got on the bus, his place in the third row behind the driver
became a memorial.

At first I didn't know he had passed away. I found out
from a heavyset young woman who was also a regular passenger on Bus 15, which goes from the Katamon neighborhood to Mt. View, and on its way, streets sitting outside are
telling stories of the inside.

"Good riddance," said the young woman after I sat down
next to her. Her name was embroidered in big letters on the

blue fabric bag lying on her lap: Nili Gonen. After a silence lasting two bus stops, she declared the name of the deceased: Baruch Glick.

She remembered how my sitting next to him started. How I once stumbled during the ride, falling on him. To make sure I didn't fall on him again, he pulled my sleeve the next day as I was passing. His gesture was clear: The seat was empty and I should sit down. For a whole week he kept pulling my sleeve, and made sure I didn't get bored on the ride. He had a need to put things in order on the bus. The driver should turn the radio up, later turn it down. He even called Nili Gonen to order. He didn't like her giggling and used to call out to her: "Lady! Lady!"

Nili told me he actually knew her name, but when angry, he tended to forget names. He didn't forget the names of drivers though, and even added titles to them. Mister Vladimir, Herr Yichya. His Hebrew, necktied with a German accent, amused her. She knew quite a lot about him. They were neighbors. Once he nearly became her stepfather. Her mother fell for him many years ago. He didn't like people falling all over him, so he got angry, forgot her name, and lived with another woman for twenty years. Two years after their wedding he forgot his wife's name too. The two never spoke to one another until the day he died.

I didn't know any of this when he was alive. On the bus we never exchanged details about one another. The bus was bustling with life: I should look and see what was going on. You could also slide open the window and let the street come in. Not in Rechavia. There all the streets were sunk in greenery and slumber. Not so in Mekor Baruch. Already at the Nathan Strauss stop, the street boarded the bus in the shape of a tall yeshiva student. I should look at how his hat touched the ceiling, his sidelocks touched his shoulders. A good-looking young Chasid. I should steal a glance at him and see how he stopped by us and continued the ride standing. At Shabbat Square, just before the bus turned onto Kings of Israel Street, the young Chasid started curling his left sidelock with both hands so that his face, without raising suspicion, was turned toward the door that would open on the next stop for Queen Esther. That's what Baruch Glick called the young woman who got on there, because of her lush beauty. Her long dress imparted vitality to every move. Folds and movements united into an orchestra, and her whole body exuded song. With a little imagination I should be able to see in the double glass of the open window the reflection of the two while she passed by the Chasid. Both he and she shrank back to avoid touch. Even the no-touch turned into music.

As the young woman continued to make her way down the aisle, the Chasid changed sidelocks. Turning his face toward the depth of the bus, he was now curling the right one with both hands, past the National Hall Building, past the warm smells of Angel Bakery, and throughout the curves and loops the bus was making along the bottom of Mt. View. At the final stop the mountains of Jerusalem filled up the windows, and the two got off the bus through separate doors, walking away together. It was then that Baruch Glick, may his memory be blessed, was hearing music in nature.

"We don't see them anymore," said Nili, and told me that Baruch Glick's wife visited her at times. Things changed at home, she told her. First there was silence, now it was quiet. Even the bus rides, in Nili's opinion, were no longer the same. The deceased's place was taken by a blabbering old man. The driver Herr Yichya retired. Mister Vladimir became religious. He put on a yarmulke, and changed the radio station from the news channel to the Living Almighty channel.

"The world is moving on," said Nili. And after a short pause added: "And so is the bus."

Under the Pressure of Time

THE WOMAN IN BLACK SITTING NEXT TO ME IN THE FRONT seat, right behind the driver of Bus 18, probably didn't imagine that during this ride I would get to hear her voice, learn her name, and that she would tell me of her own free will a long story in just a few words. When I got on the bus, still in Kiryat Yovel, she wasn't at all pleased at my sitting down next to her. Her reactions were abrupt. She moved the basket from her lap to the window side, immediately making an imaginary space between her and me: Let no sleeve touch a sleeve, no trouser leg touch her long skirt. A golden toenail peeked out from the sandal on the foot closest to me.

I accepted my lot and out of laziness didn't look for another seat. At the next stop it was already too late to change my mind. The bus filled up with passengers who were jammed along the aisle and on the steps. A female soldier who didn't pay attention to the driver's warning to watch out for the door managed to push herself in, but her bag got caught outside the closed door. It flapped in the wind, hitting the hinge of the transparent door. The passengers standing close to her sympathized with her distress. The driver should open the door! A tall guy with a ponytail, who also pushed himself in, actually praised the driver for not getting excited by the calls. In his opinion it was about time citizens, including soldiers, learned to obey rules.

The woman next to me remained outside this commotion. Nearly frozen, she didn't react when the door opened slightly and the bag was pulled in. And she didn't react when the ponytailed guy suddenly stopped praising the driver and started condemning him. A motorcyclist cut in front of the bus, which stopped suddenly. The standing passengers bumped into one another. Even those who were seated were jolted. The tall guy hit his head. Now he was angry not only at the driver but also at the government. His anger lasted several stops and did not subside even when the bus stopped at the Agron and Queen Shlomzion intersection. In the front window a large billboard announced the construction of a new neighborhood: the City of David.

Throughout this time the woman next to me didn't show any change. Under a thin layer of frost she guarded her silence and the imaginary space between us, even though it too suffered a jolt. I was touched by her silence and decided to listen to it when she too was startled, as if by a sudden stop. She called out toward the other bus that stood alongside ours at the traffic light:

"Aliza! Aliza! Why didn't you come to the funeral?"

Aliza was sitting in the front seat closest to the door, and her window was parallel to ours. Outside, the mirrors of the two buses nearly touched one another. The soldier had by now moved further into the bus, but the tall guy remained standing near the driver. He bent slightly, trying to see this Aliza who hadn't been at the funeral. A tower-shaped earring dangled from Aliza's right ear along her neck, reflecting in the mirror of our bus.

"Carmella?! Carmella?! How was it there?" Aliza's voice rang out above the noises of the intersection. Two of her fingers were playing with the earring, and she turned her ear to listen to the details while the stoplight remained red.

I too turned my ear. Even though the red light was threatening to change, I had no doubt Carmella would overcome it and tell all. I once met a man who, between the red and green, told me his whole life story. This time, though, I was wrong. In vain did Carmella fill up with desire to tell Aliza all. By the time she raised a leg, moved the basket, and brought her mouth closer to the window, the light changed and the other bus hurried off passing us by.

When our bus moved on, Carmella noticed me and considered from the corner of her eye whether it was worth her while to tell me what Aliza wanted to know. She didn't have anyone else. Even the tall guy was already deeper in the bus.

Aliza disappeared, I thought to myself, but the desire to tell was still there, and the story wasn't lost. Carmella would tell. Now, even time worked in her favor. There was no red light threat, and there was still a long way to go. Ahead of us was King David Street, the Bell Park, Emeck Refaim. And when these disappeared behind us, I pinned my hopes on Derech Hebron. But before we saw Cleopatra Restaurant at the Ein Gedi intersection, Carmella pressed the stop button.

A sleeve touched a sleeve, a trouser leg touched a skirt,

and my hopes vanished. I stood up to let her pass, and was sorry for Aliza who was gone and the story that was lost. Carmella waited for the door to open, and descending the steps, she looked back at me, the gold of the toenail twinkled in her eyes, and in six soft words she described the funeral Aliza didn't attend:

"It was not like his wedding."

Reflections

I N THE GLASS AT THE BUS STOP ON PROPHET ISAIAH
Street, across from the former Edison Cinema, I saw my
own reflection staring at a beautiful woman who was waiting
for Bus 9. I didn't know my ears were so big. I shrugged and
closed the eye that was side-glancing at the tall woman so I
wouldn't be tempted to tell her straight out how she looked.

Earlier I sneaked a glance when she leaned over the baby
in the stroller and uttered endearments in a sweet voice.

"My little Sonny," she called to him

I turned away from the glass to drive the two reflections
out of my sight, and looked across the street toward the Edison Cinema. In its early days the Edison was also a theater,
but now it was standing desolate and abandoned. The three
grand entrances sealed by boards, most of its windows bro-

ken. One of them still held a movie poster. A bare-legged actress smiling. The woman beside me was wearing a long skirt past her ankles. Without looking again at her reflection, I mumbled to myself that she wasn't any less beautiful than the Hollywood actress. I wouldn't tell her that. I gave out a compliment once, and failed. I climbed four flights of stairs and knocked on the door of a famous poet in order to praise her to her face. She invited me in and three minutes later kicked me out. I hadn't praised her enough.

I wasn't going to take another chance. I stepped away from the bus stop so I wouldn't be tempted. I walked up the street toward Shabbat Square, and stretched my neck. Perhaps I'd notice a bus coming, and if it was Bus 15 I'd get on and stop mumbling about the two beautiful women.

I began mumbling as soon as she got to the bus stop. She wanted to know if Bus 9 had already passed. She was in a hurry to get to a family reunion at The Belgium House on the university campus. She was actually talking to herself and to the baby in the stroller. I just listened in and inadvertently became a partner to her tension and rush.

Now I returned to the bus stop, shook my head and said that no bus was coming. I didn't want her to be late to the reunion. A large family, relatives and sons of relatives from all over the country and elsewhere, not to mention the ones in Jerusalem.

"Generations of them," she said and wanted to know whether I too was a Jerusalemite.

"Hardly twelve years," I answered.

Her beautiful face froze for a moment, and she passed her look from me to my reflection in the glass. I too turned my look there, and once again was surprised by my big ears.

"Bus 9," I called to her joyfully. I helped her, pulling up the stroller through the back door, and before I was able to get off, the door closed behind me. The bus moved on, and we both remained standing face to face exchanging a smile that was slowly fading away. Before it faded completely I told her how she looked. "Beautiful like a Swedish movie star!"

"More than that," she answered and locked the stroller wheels with her foot. She didn't give me time to wonder. She freed a hand, raised it, and immediately added: "Eight generations in Jerusalem!"

Once again the compliment failed, and I had no choice but to shrink away and softly peep that I too wasn't a new object. But where were my generations? By her beautiful countenance, it was clear that anyone born outside the realm of Jerusalem had no generations. I was looking for my reflection in the bus window. In vain. From whence shall my help come?[1] I mumbled.

She leaned over to me and revealed that for a long time these very words didn't leave her lips. She was unable to conceive, and when she lost hope she went abroad, found a baby and adopted him. I should peek in the stroller and see how much he looked like her. I didn't have time because the bus stopped, the door opened, and I got off to look for a Bus 15 stop. The woman quickly took her baby out of the stroller, lifted him for me to see through the closed door, and before the bus moved on, she mouthed to me clearly:

"The ninth generation in Jerusalem!"

My Neighbor from Guiloh

O N BUS 32 A BACHELOR FROM MOSCOW, A FORMER
neighbor of mine, called out to me:
"Getting married!"

Sitting in the back, he spotted me getting on the bus in
the city's center, taking a seat behind the driver. Now that
the bus was emptying, he pushed his way past the few passengers still standing in the aisle, and wanted to know if I
received the invitation to his wedding. The driver threw a
weary glance at him, fixed the yarmulke on his head, and
continued to drive. I moved over to the window, making
room for him so he could tell me the details. We hadn't seen
one another since I left the neighborhood some three years
earlier. In those days he used to complain that so long as he
lived in this neighborhood he had no chance of getting mar-

ried. Because of the neighbors. What respectable woman would want to live there, he used to ask me.

He didn't sit down. The bus was coming to the end of its route, and he suggested that since we were lucky to meet, I should come along with him to see the changes in his apartment.

We used to live next door to one another, and meet on the stairs by the dumpsters at the backyard, and also in his apartment whenever he brought in a new piece of decoration. He decorated the house for a respectable woman. A cabinet from Moscow, its shiny wood and glass keeping up with the large mirror across. Crystals inside the cabinet. Long-stemmed wine glasses and stemless vodka glasses. A nude Hollywood actress took up half a wall, and a nude of himself like the statue of David in Florence took up the other half. But who's the young girl who'd want to marry him and live among neighbors who used to live in caves? Nobody in Moscow ever knew of their existence. Here they surrounded him and kept behaving like cave dwellers.

He used to sit in a café on Ben Yehuda Street, gazing at passing girls, marking the ones he liked. He knew his worth: an academic woman, five foot five, no less.

Once, when we were having coffee at his house, he caught me glancing at the large mirror, surveying the three cities it reflected — Moscow, Florence, Hollywood. He nodded and said I should mark his words. No young woman from Ben Yehuda Street would ever join the three cities in the mirror. Since he was a man of principle he was doomed to remain a bachelor for the rest of his life.

Now, after we got off the bus and turned toward his home, I could see that sticking to his principles had paid off. He did find a woman to his liking.

The neighborhood's little shopping center hadn't changed much. The grocery owner placed a table and three chairs in front of the store, and added a sign: "The Corner Café."

The shoemaker's shop turned into a flower shop but the sign remained: "Aaron Soleveichik — Shoemaker." Three men with baseball caps were playing cards, standing on a small lawn. My own name, half-erased, remained stuck on the mailbox at the building's entrance.

We ran up the stairs to the third floor. He made coffee in the kitchen and I walked around his apartment. The nudes from Hollywood and Florence were gone. Their place was taken by framed paintings that reflected in the large mirror. Red and yellow patches, foggy mountains, caves with paths between them, bird-sized people.

"They're hers," he said.

We drank coffee, and he told me she was painting the landscape of her homeland.

On leaving, I scratched off the other half of my name from the mailbox. When I got to the bus stop, the same driver who brought me here was waiting for me, having managed to complete a full round, there and back. As I got on the bus, he threw me a double look, fixed the yarmulke on his head, asked and also answered:

"Getting married?"

"Getting married!"

Portrait of a Line at a Bus Stop

I LEFT MY HOUSE TO BE AMONG PEOPLE. I JOINED A LINE for a bus at Jaffa Street, near Mahaneh Yehuda Market. The good-looking woman who joined behind me sighed in relief for not having missed the bus. Thank God the bus was late too. She put her baskets down and asked for the exact time. I pushed up my sleeve, showed her my watch, and continued listening to the two men standing in front of me, talking about food and death. The taller one said the three rich meals he was eating daily were his death, and his short companion asked:

"Why?"

I pulled my sleeve back down, looked at the woman who was still happy, and I too was happy, even though I wasn't waiting for the bus and had no intention of getting on one.

Actually, I very much wanted the bus to be late so I could hear why the tall man was going to die soon. He was about fifty with a belly and bald head. Five years ago, he said, it wasn't like that. He used to work like a donkey, eat like a dog, and was healthy like an ox. The trouble started when he switched jobs. He was lucky to get one at an American plant, and his good luck was also his bitter end.

"Why?" asked his short companion. I took a quick glance at the street and sighed in relief. Thank God the approaching bus wasn't ours. It passed without stopping.

The good-looking woman, however, started showing signs of disappointment, and once again wanted to know the exact time. Bus 18, she thought, was the worst city bus. She knew what she was talking about. Ten years of personal experience. She took this bus daily. I asked her if she was also taking other buses, and she answered angrily:

"Why would I do that! Of course not."

She drew out a red-nailed finger and declared that for this bus there's a driver who's later than the others. She had additional complaints:

"What kind of country is this?"

The happy feeling I adopted from her earlier, and the

curiosity I borrowed from the short companion, also raised
my interest in the tardy driver. But the woman grew silent,
so I turned my ear to the clear voice of the belly-and-bald
guy. I didn't miss a word despite the constant noise coming
from the street and market. Americans knew how to eat, said
the man. The meals in the plant were excellent and rich in
meat, three times a day. The doctor warned him more than
once to stop eating those darn meals.

"Why?" asked the short guy. His voice sounded clear
despite the rattle of the bus that had just stopped, a double-
length Bus 18. Three doors opened wide. The woman collected her baskets in a hurry. The bus finally arrived, but her
contentment was long gone and her anger grew stronger.
She would show the tardy driver she was right. The world
should know what kind of a country we live in. Determined
to push herself in, she leapt past the two men talking about
food and death. I became worried I might not get to hear the
dying man's answer.

When the woman was already inside, one of her baskets
turned over, and a boy was helping her collect the oranges
that rolled out of it. The tall man used these few seconds to
explain to his short companion why he didn't listen to the

doctor's advice and was unable to resist temptation. He laid his hands on his companion's shoulders and shouted to his face:

"They give these meals for free, man. It's all free!"

The three doors closed. The bus moved on. The line was gone. I remained alone, leaning against a light pole, waiting for a new line to start.

The Man from the Bus

H E DIDN'T RECOGNIZE ME, THE HATMAKER FROM MEA Shearim, when I approached him in one of the court-yards of the Ungarin Houses. I took another look at the slip of paper I was holding, and compared it with the faded letters on the sign hanging lopsided above his workshop: "Reuven Tzeinwirt — Hittlemacher." He stood at the doorway, the flaps of his two coats wide open. To his right, there was a short, big-belly wine barrel made of wood and metal bands, which he had gotten for the synagogue dinner he'd invited me to. Like the barrel, he too was short, yellow and round.

"I'm the man from the bus!" I called to him.

We rode together on Bus 5 to visit women in the maternity ward at the Sha'arey Zedek Hospital. He was sitting near me, surrounded by his five little girls. The eldest of them, about ten, wouldn't let go of him until he told her the names of the two new girls momma had just given birth to.

The hatmaker sucked on a curl from his beard and refused to remember me. My light-colored clothes weren't to his taste in his own neighborhood, and my hat, a goy's hat, embarrassed him. But on the bus on the way to the hospital, and later in the spacious elevator, and especially in the maternity ward when the doctor asked the visitors to step out awhile, and we found ourselves face to face at the end of a dimly lit corridor — we were exchanging blessings, congratulations, quotations from the sages, and a few details about our daily lives. He told me all his seven daughters were from his present wife, his third. With the first one he lived five years, with the second a little less. Between the first and the second there was a five-year period, and twice as much had to pass before his luck turned with the third one. Then and only then was he able to prove to the world he was right. His two previous wives were flat like boards with nothing to hold, neither the one nor the other, though both of them claimed he wasn't man enough.

I took money out of my pocket and waved it at him to let

him know I came to buy a black hat. But Reuven Tzeinwirt locked the door, rolled down the shades.

"Go! Go away!" he said and accompanied his words with little hand movements.

With his look he brushed away the money in my hand. The guests were about to appear any minute. He didn't want to be seen with me when they came to get the wine barrel for the synagogue dinner. Perhaps they were already waiting at the synagogue.

"Blood libel," he told me in the cool corridor of the hospital.[1] The neighbors believed his previous wives and wouldn't listen to him. For nine years he was an outcast, a leper. In later years, however, with every new birth he proved to them what a terrible injustice they had done to him. And now he was giving them double proof. He stretched his hands forward like an orchestra conductor and called out:

"Twin girls!" With a soft, confident voice, he added that everyone would now come to the feast. To eat and drink and burst with envy.

Reuven Tzeinwirt approached the wine barrel, tucked the wings of his coats into the belt below his belly, and both he and the barrel stood like twins in the yellowish light of the setting sun, waiting to be taken to the synagogue. But no one came. Two men in black were whispering on a steep stairway, their backs turned to us. A boy dug into a dumpster, pulled out a rag, scrunched it into a ball and kicked it. A passing woman threw a hostile look at me. Reuven Tzeinwirt's hostility also didn't go away. He didn't like my shaven face. When I turned to leave, he pointed at the barrel and wondered at the guests who were taking their time.

Since I was already there, perhaps I could help him roll it to the synagogue.

We rolled the barrel from courtyard to courtyard, the sound of its rolling echoed in the silence between the houses. The men in black continued to whisper on the steep stairway. The hostile woman disappeared. The boy with the rag-ball also disappeared. We both continued to roll the barrel. Twice we crossed underneath laundry hanging from a line stretched between two houses. We lifted the barrel up three steps and placed it at the entrance of the synagogue. We breathed and smiled in relief. The sun continued to set, the houses around us sunk further into silence. The smile we exchanged softened Tzeinwirt's hostility, and he asked me to stay and receive with him the guests who were coming to the feast.

They'd drink and dance. The entire neighborhood and its houses would come out dancing.

And he was right. His own family was coming toward us: His stout wife carrying the twin girls in her arms, surrounded by the fiery red-headed girls. The setting sun lit up the color of their hair, and freckles spilled abundantly over their long flowery dresses. They came toward their father in a skipping that turned into a dance and Tzeinwirt skipped down the three steps. The houses also didn't stand still. Back in the dimly lit corridor of the hospital the hatmaker promised me that's how it would be: the neighborhood would dance like rams, the houses like young sheep.[2]

About Patches and Bears

S HE CAME TO VISIT ME ON BUS 9, AND IN CASE I DIDN'T recognize her — we hadn't seen each other for sixty years — she quickly introduced herself:

"Chaveleh the sock mender."

In Chaveleh's mind I remained the same thirteen-year-old boy who could keep a secret, and she remained in mine the old spinster, twenty-nine-years-old, sitting on a worn bench at the far end of the backyard, stretching a torn sock over the rim of a cup and cross-stitching it.

Chaveleh's patches were famous in our little town in Poland. She even mended the torn socks of the town's rich man and his family. She once made me a patch shaped as a flying bird, and for the rich man's son, a student in Paris, she made a dancing bear.

She saw the dancing bear in the market when she was taking back mended socks. She wanted to pet the bear, but didn't have a penny to pay the Gypsy. The rich man's son happened to pass by and offered her a penny for a kiss. They kissed, and she petted the bear.

The very next day she was all too ready to go back to the market and pet the bear again, but after the first kiss in her life she felt her dress was too shabby and too long, covering her ankles. If only she had a different dress, one that showed her knees, she wouldn't hesitate.

Her hesitation grew in the days that followed. When she got a new bunch of torn socks from the rich man's house, she found out from the maid which one of them was the rich man's son's, and made a dancing-bear patch for him.

His name was Simon even though in town they called him Shimon. Once Simon wore the sock, he'd understand the sign and would come to the backyard to kiss her again.

But her dream for a kiss went hand in hand with her anxiety over the shabby dress. She'd run and hide away as soon as he'd appear at the low entrance to the backyard. From her place on the worn bench she noticed that even small people had to bend down when entering the yard, and in the market

Simon was the tallest of them all. He'd have to bend very low, and she'd have time to hide away in the yard.

People entering the backyard made her heart leap. Even when it was the rich man's maid who one day brought a new bunch of torn socks, not even one of them Simon's.

"He returned to Paris," said the maid.

"He'll send a postcard," Chaveleh told me. She knew I could keep a secret. When the postcard arrives I'd read it to her and wouldn't tell a soul. She wished she herself could tell one letter from another. Since she couldn't, she made me a bird patch and we both started waiting for the Polish postman who'd bend at the entrance even though he was very small, would straighten up in the yard, wave the postcard in his right hand, and call out her name.

"Eva!" the postman would call, for in Paris they change one's name.

But very rarely did the Polish postman cross the low entrance. Once he brought a letter from New York. Another time from Australia. A postcard from Paris he didn't bring.

One day when I joined her on the worn bench, Chaveleh told me: "Here." With moist eyes she pointed at something hidden in her bosom and continued:

"A postcard."

Even here, on the bus, her eyes were moist. She knew this bus was crossing the city, connecting the two parts of the university. She also knew that times have changed, that no one was mending torn socks anymore, and that there weren't any dancing bears in the markets. She asked that we whisper, so no one could hear us.

The postcard she then took out of her bosom hadn't been from Simon. It was a stamped postcard addressed to him. She had gotten it from the maid in exchange for free sock mending. Let the maid keep the mending payment for herself.

Chaveleh smoothed out the folds, for the postcard arrived folded. Now we only had to erase what the rich man's wife wrote to her son, and write to him in a clear handwriting something about a dancing bear and a second kiss.

We were both excited when I sat down next to her with the eraser in my hand. Once again she drew the postcard from her bosom, and I erased. The eraser wore out, the writing remained.

Chaveleh continued to keep the postcard in her bosom. From time to time I joined her, hoping this time the ink might come off. So long as we kept trying, she said, there was hope for a second kiss. She'd also write for him to send her colorful fabric for a pretty dress. Then she wouldn't be ashamed to come out from the yard and go for a walk in the market. She heard that once again a Gypsy came to town.

Here in Jerusalem, when the bus was approaching its last stop, Chaveleh asked that we stop talking. Let's be silent and think about things that are gone and those that are not, and together mourn over patches and bears.

The Broom

THE THREE OF US GOT ON BUS 20 AND RODE FROM IR
Ganim to the Jaffa Gate[1] of the Old City. The other two,
a lieutenant-general from the Air Force and an Australian
reporter who hated Jews, sat facing me, knees touching
knees. I reminded them who I was, the man who when
young swore to be a proud Jew in body and soul.

The two didn't know one another. I visited the military
airbase commander right after I immigrated to Israel and
became a shepherd in a nearby kibbutz. I met Thomas
Brown when I invited myself to his house in Melbourne after
World War II, following an anti-Semitic essay he wrote in
The Age, the Victoria State newspaper.

In those days everyone in the small Jewish community
of Melbourne thought it was their duty to be proud Jews. I

knew how to be proud in body. I walked with my head held high. But how would I know when the soul was lifting up its head? I was hoping it would happen at Thomas Brown's house. I'd mention in our conversation a few impressive names: Moses. King David. Prophet Isaiah. Albert Einstein. And he'd change his mind.

I did it. He promised to change direction in his next essay. But he didn't, and my soul didn't lift its head.

Thomas Brown wasn't comfortable on the bus. He couldn't remember when he last used public transportation. He arrived in Israel toward the end of the millennium in order to follow in the footsteps of Jesus Christ. He tracked me down in Jerusalem and we arranged to take a short trip in the city. His opinion of the Jewish people still hadn't changed. In Australia, he said, time didn't do much. Even at our first and only meeting in his house he found me ridiculous. A sort of spiritual plumber on a mission to repair broken pipes in the darkness of his soul.

Here on the bus Thomas Brown took an interest in the densely packed apartment buildings along the streets of Ir Ganim, of Kiryat Yovel. In the laundry hanging on the balconies. At the Mahaneh Yehuda stop, when the bus filled up with basket-carrying travelers, he got up and gave his seat to a heavyset woman with heavy baskets. He himself got pushed toward the back of the long bus, gesturing to me that when we got to Jaffa Gate, he'd walk alone on The Via Dolorosa.[2] He'd measure every step of the way and would ponder the message the Son of God bestowed upon humanity: Love for humankind.

The lieutenant-general also didn't feel comfortable on the bus. He was annoyed by the heavy basket the woman next to him placed on his knees. Nowadays he was a neighbor of mine in Jerusalem, and joined the ride at the last moment. He asked me not to mention his name in the story, and told me that whenever he happened to get to Jaffa Gate, he too felt a need to go alone to the Wailing Wall. A beard and moustache, both of the same thickness, were still decorating his face, joining around the mouth into a zero. Now, facing me, it was a graying zero. Back then when I visited him at the airport, it was a pure orange zero.

The zero didn't prevent me then from laying out to him, in great length, the issue of grazing pastures. To him too I mentioned some impressive names: Moses, King David, Prophet Amos. All of them shepherds. I requested permission to enter the field next to the airport runway. I'd lead the herd with my head held high, and perhaps my soul too would finally lift its head up.

The commander also found me ridiculous. He waited patiently for me to finish my speech, and when I didn't stop, he gave a long silent yawn. Seeing before me two zeros, one inside the other, I took a breath and fell silent for a moment. The commander took advantage of this moment to tell me he'd let me lead the herd around the airport's pastures only if instead of dropping impressive names I should come equipped with a broom. He himself was once a shepherd, and knew what happened when a herd of sheep crossed the runway in panic. The runway must stay clean, he added. I shouldn't leave behind even one black bean.

The next morning before sunrise, I set out with the herd toward the airport, my head held high, holding the biggest broom I could get my hands on in a nearby town. With the key he gave me I unlocked a side gate. When the sheep finished crossing over to the pasture, the runway was covered with a broad carpet of excrement, and my body was covered with sweat.

Bus 20 reached its final stop by the Old City, and I saw

the commander and the reporter walking each on his own separate way. One toward The Via Dolorosa, the other toward the Wailing Wall.

I stayed behind and walked around in the alleys, recalling that sweaty morning on the runway. Against the background of a rising sun and noise of combat jets, with a broom in my hands, a body bent down and a head facing the ground, the soul lifted its head up.

The Fifth Smile

IT WASN'T TO REST THAT I SAT DOWN ON THE BENCH, AND it wasn't to go anywhere, but to get a closer look at the blind man and his dagger-like sideburns. Dressed in a black pullover sweater he was sitting on a hot day at a Jaffa Street bus stop. There were three seats on the plastic bench, and the blind man was sitting in the middle. As I sat down to his right a bus stopped, and the driver announced his route. Even before it stopped, the driver noticed the man's dark glasses and cane. He opened the door and called toward him:

"27!"

The man didn't react. He remained absorbed within himself, dozing. From up close his sideburns got even sharper.

I once took care of a blind old man who groomed similar

sideburns. After shaving he used to feel them, and was glad to find them intact. Rudolph was his name.

Another bus stopped. Its driver also announced his route. 36. No one got off, no one got on. I watched the driver stretching his neck toward the open door and waiting hesitantly. Perhaps the blind man would hear his voice and wake up from his nap. The door closed, the bus moved on, engulfing us in the heat wave it left behind. The blind man didn't react, as if under a spell of depression.

Rudolph too had moments of depression. He used to sit in the lobby of the nursing home where he lived, quiet and reserved. There were also other residents who spent most of the day sitting in the lobby. When one of them saw that I was coming and announced me, Rudolph would burst out laughing. He had a youthful voice, and his laughter was also youthful.

I got up from the bench and glanced at the bus-stop sign to count the number of bus lines that stopped there. After the blind man wouldn't get on the third bus, line 41, I knew I wasn't moving away until all the other lines passed by: 11, 25, 48, 171, 173, 174, 175.

Now I also glanced at the young woman who sat down

on the blind man's left. All neck and legs: a blouse with low horizon, mini-skirt with a rising landscape. I didn't stop at only one glance. When I returned to my seat and a fourth bus passed without the blind man budging, I stole another glance at the young woman — and realized I'm not the only onlooker. The blind man also peeked at her. Through an opening between the dark glasses and cheekbone, his left eye found a free path to leap and skip through. From my angle he looked as if he were scanning the day's news in a newspaper spread out before him. Headlines only. A headline on the left, a headline on the right, and between them an imaginary arrow pulling the eye down toward a piece of news at the bottom of the page.

I tapped him lightly and asked if he was going anywhere. He didn't answer, his sharpened sideburns kept threatening.

After I'd pass my fingers along blind Rudolph's sideburns and find them fit for going out, his rolling laughter would infect the other residents with smiles. A woman once told me how far Rudolph's laughter rolled: From Rudolph to the hunchback, from the hunchback to her depressed husband, and from her husband to herself. Then she too smiled.

Another bus arrived and the young woman disappeared

into it. I remained close to the blind man and told him what the woman who was infected by her husband's smile told me: I became her fourth smile

The blind man passed his cane from one hand to the other, raised his dark glasses to his forehead, and presented me a business card he took out of a small pocket in his black sweater. I should read what's written there: Classic Actor. Philosopher. Odessa, Ukraine.

He asked me if I'd ever learned Torah and remembered what God told our forefather Abraham. A spark lit up in his eyes and his sideburns didn't threaten anymore.

"Go, get thee away," I answered.

He raised his right hand and pointed at some distant point in the direction of the tall Kellal Building, toward the Mahaneh Yehuda Market.

I got up and stretched, and while I was hesitating which direction to take, another young woman took my seat on the plastic bench. When line 173 went on its way and the young woman remained seated on the bench, the blind man wiped a tear and returned cane, glasses, and business card, prop by prop, to their places. He sent me a fifth smile and started reviewing the new headlines, this time to his right.

The Bus Line Finisher

THE PASSENGER SITTING NEXT TO ME WAS COMPLAINING about his dead wife. Recently she came into his dream and was causing him shame. We were on Bus 25 that was going to Neveh Yaakov. When it reached its final stop it was already dark outside, and both of us, the widower and I, were the only passengers left. We were sitting in the back row, and the driver looked at us in the mirror above his head and motioned with his hand that we should get off. There was nowhere to get off to. The widower motioned with his own hand that we were going back.

We parted in the center of the city, on Prophets Street at the Davidka Square stop. The widower didn't know my name and he also didn't tell me his. He told me other details. On the bus he told me that after waking up in the middle of the night, he remained sitting in bed, legs down. He didn't even hurry to the bathroom. Just followed pieces of the dream. His wife was making love there to a young doctor. The same doctor who treated him.

When she was still alive, she accompanied him to the urology department at Hadassah Ein Karem Hospital. The doctor asked him if he still had erections. Didn't wait for an answer and wrote down in the file: "No" — then took a look at the wife, and added a period.

The widower took out of his pocket a picture of his wife, so that I too should have a look at her. He wondered at the young doctor with the black mustache. What did he find in her, the old woman? And he wondered at his wife. Already seven months in the grave, and this was what she had on her mind? He himself was mourning her every day. Dressing up — a formal suit — as on the day of her funeral, getting on a city bus, and finishing a line there and back.

On the day after the dream he finished a line there and back to the Mount of Rest. He planned what he'd tell her when he stood by her grave. He'd tell her about the dream. But he didn't. He told her about a passenger he met on the bus that took him there. She sat across from him and was impressed by his clothes. He had good taste, she said. Everything in calm brown. The hat, the tie, even the shoes and socks. She noticed, as he sat down across from her, how he carefully pulled up pant leg by pant leg in order to keep the *kneitch*, the crease along the pant leg. The creases indeed remained intact. Straight and sharp like a knife, as on the day of the funeral. She was sure he was a tourist from Romania. Only they, she said, knew how to dress.

The widower also didn't tell his wife he decided to change doctors. He'd no longer go have a look at the black mustache, which was soft as silk. In the dream the young doctor had long sideburns, they too of black silk.

We started talking about the doctor and the creases even before the ride, at the bus stop. The widower suggested that I join him on his bus so that he'd be able to tell me the dream in detail. He'd also tell me about the two ultrasounds at the clinic on Nathan Straus Street. The new doctor, a urologist without any mustache, sent him there.

He came to the clinic all dressed up as at the funeral, so that right afterwards he'd be able to finish a bus line. When he lay on the narrow table in the dark room, and the female doctor told him to pull down his pants — not much, just a little — he managed to take them off completely, and by the time the doctor turned back, he had them lying on his thighs across the table, in order to keep the creases.

To the second ultrasound, in the same month, he came in old pants, without creases, so as not to embarrass the doctor again, and so she wouldn't recognize him. But she did recognize him. Before he closed the door behind him, he heard what she said to her assistant.

The widower pressed the stop button and said: "Guess what she recognized me by." I used this moment to give him back his wife's picture. She didn't look old. It was a picture of a twenty-year-old woman. Long braids, long legs. That's what she looked like in the dream, when she was making love to the young doctor. Her legs — they were the reason he was running away from there. Didn't want to see what they were both doing in his bed. Ran away from the dream and got lost in the crowd.

When we got off the bus, the widower put the picture back into his pocket, and before he disappeared into the dark alley he told me what the doctor recognized him by. The picture of his bladder.

Sausage in Honey

O N OUR SECOND ENCOUNTER I ALREADY KNEW ABOUT
the old man who returned home, and the name of the
passenger who told me about him: Yocheved.

On both occasions we met on Bus 27, which was going
between Hadassah Ein Karem Hospital and the Wailing
Wall. In both places Yocheved looked for help: with the doctor and with God. From the latter, she said, she'd been lately
disappointed.

She was telling me this as we were sitting in the first row,
and the bus had already left the hospital grounds.

In Hadassah we took the same elevator up, and the same
elevator down. On the way down we were no longer
strangers. The few seconds going up and down pulled
threads of acquaintance between us.

As the bus picked up speed downhill, and the view in the window opened its eyes, Yocheved told me why she was disappointed by way of a fable and its lesson, which stretched along the streets of Hantke, Herzl, Jaffa, until the Wall.

If I were a doctor with two patients, a man and a dog, having to choose which one of them to cure — the man or the dog — which one of them would I have chosen?

Yocheved didn't expect me to answer. The doctor from Hadassah told her the answer was obvious. But unlike him, what did God do? He made fun of His own justice. The man in the fable was her husband, and the dog belonged to the grocery shop below. The husband and the dog got sick at the same time. The dog threw up and got well. Her husband threw up and died.

It was then that the old man came into the scene. After the funeral, in the evening, she didn't turn on the television. She also didn't turn on the light. As she was sitting alone in the dark, she noticed a window with light in the opposite building. An old man was moving around there in the room.

She moved her chair closer to the window and watched the man making himself a meal: pouring tea, slicing bread. He also sliced sausage and dipped the slices in honey. Every slice had a strand of honey pulling back into the jar. She never heard of such a mixture. When the old man turned off the light, she too went to sleep.

Next morning, when she was making herself something to eat, she found herself thinking of the sausage and honey, and of the old man. She learned about him from the woman who owned the grocery shop, who came up to see her during shiva. The old man was a long-time neighbor. Lately he started avoiding people he knew. When seeing an acquaintance coming toward him, he would turn away and be gone.

Yocheved and her husband were also long-time neighbors, but she didn't remember having ever met the old man. While her husband was alive, she never paid attention to the light in the window.

She also didn't pay attention to the noises on the bus and outside of it, to the sudden stops and traffic jams. She and her husband came from the Holocaust. They both lost their families. They didn't have children of their own. They had met on their way to Israel, and got married on the way. At first they had some jobs here and there. Later they quit their jobs and lived off of the monthly compensation they received from Germany. She suffered from diabetes and obesity, and her husband from asthma. When he started coughing she'd boil water and he'd breathe the vapor. She kept in the refrigerator slices of uncooked potatoes she used to put on the back of his neck. Neither the old man nor his window were ever on their minds.

The old man dipped slices of sausage in honey the following evening too. He dipped sausage in honey throughout shiva. And he kept doing it afterwards as well. She couldn't stop herself any longer. The temptation was too strong. She bought honey, she bought sausage, and waited for the dark. That evening the old man's window remained dark too. She felt like tasting the dish, but she didn't. A week went by and the window remained dark. They told her in the grocery shop that the old man moved to a nursing home.

When the bus approached the Old City, Yocheved opened her big bag, took out a jar of honey, took out a sausage wrapped in a plastic bag, and asked me what she could do with them. She brought them all the way to Hadassah to ask the doctor if she could have a tiny bit of sausage in just a drop of honey. Not even a whole slice. Once again the doctor told her the answer was obvious. The sausage would increase her weight, the honey her blood sugar.

When she put the honey and sausage back into her bag, a piece of paper fell out of it. I picked it up and saw a photocopy of the kaddish. During shiva she made many copies of it, to be put in the cracks of the Wall, each saying a kaddish for her husband.

I accompanied her all the way from the final stop to the Wailing Wall Square, since she wanted to know what I was doing for a living. She couldn't believe I was walking the streets, getting on and off buses, trying to find out what was going on with human beings.

On our second encounter Yocheved was again going to put a kaddish in the Wall. She had a different hair style. Her white hair was rising wave upon wave above her forehead. When we took seats in the front row, she nodded and whispered:

"The old man's back, and there's light in the window."

The Substitute

THE WOMAN ON THE BUS AND THE RABBIT IN THE FIELD provided me with a quick answer on television. I was invited to the studio on a moment's notice for a live talk on Jerusalem Day.[1] The TV hostess received me with an irritated politeness. She was angry at the poet M.E., whom she was supposed to have this talk with, and he let her down. He got sick and didn't show up. Some of her anger at him she aimed at me, his substitute, and with quick sweeping movements sent me off to makeup.

Her own makeup brought out her beauty. Young, tall, waves of hair. Her face — all eyes. She called me, mispronouncing my name, and asked that we don't waste time. While I was getting made-up I should prepare a few words, a very short sentence as an opener. For when the cue was given, she'd present me with a very short question as a warm-up:

"What does Jerusalem do to you?"

When the cue was given, the hostess leaped at once from King David, the founder of the City some three thousand years ago, to me, this time without mispronouncing my name. She shot her question hurriedly and the camera now focused on me.

The first time I saw a picture of King David was through a peephole of a box covered with black cloth. He was sitting on a throne with the Book of Psalms lying on his lap. He looked thoughtful, and the book, with enlarged letters, was open to the verse, "From whence shall my help come?"[2]

The young woman on the bus two days ago displayed a similar distress. She was sitting behind me, telling the woman next to her all the shameful things that happened to her last year. Though her voice was pleasant, you could hear that she too like King David needed help.

And so did the white rabbit, some thirty years ago, when I saw it standing behind a bush in a small carrot patch in the Valley of Jezreel. It perked its ears and stayed close to the bush not to be noticed. It had nowhere to go. My herd of sheep was scattered all over the area. They crowded around the bushes in groups. The summer sun was about to set. It was quiet all around, a sheep moved from one bush to another, the donkey wagged its tail. As the sun lowered, the shadow of the rabbit's ears grew longer.

The story of the young woman on the bus also grew longer. She spoke without pause along five stops through the center of Jerusalem. When the bus entered some shade, I caught sight of her listener's reflection in the window. She lent her ear to her companion. My own ears grew longer, like the shadow of the rabbit's ears in the setting sun.

The hostess was waiting for a prompt, short answer. With a mute hand's gesture, she wanted to know why I kept silent, and moved a wave of hair from her forehead to her ear.

The owner of the peephole box in the little Polish town of Biala wore a red hat with a feather sticking out. He had placed his box on a one-foot stand. When the penny's worth of viewing time was over, the king disappeared. When the sun in the valley finished setting, darkness swallowed the shadow of the rabbit's ears. By the fifth stop of the bus, at the Jaffa-Straus and King George intersection, the girl stopped talking. But then, after a brief silence, I heard the hushed voice of her companion. Had my ears not turned into long shadows in the dark, I wouldn't have caught her words. She called her name quietly, and whispered her question:

"Arnona, from all that you've told me, didn't it swap out your head?"

I repeated the hostess's very short question — what does Jerusalem do to me? — and I saw on her face, all waves and eyes, that she too was relieved when she heard my very short answer:

"Jerusalem? Every single day it swaps out my head."

How a Story Gets Cooking

I TOLD MYSELF TO KEEP AWAY FROM STORIES FOR A WHILE, both telling and writing. I didn't keep my word. Again and again I found myself telling and writing. It usually started with something trivial, like the hand of a distant relative from Odessa. He left a message on my answering machine — that he made Aliyah, was living in Ashkelon, and was coming to visit with his new wife.

I was living then on Zungvil Street in Kiryat Yovel, in a big apartment building, and my home was nothing but a tiny apartment. People who came over for the first time were warned to approach the building slowly, in case they passed through my apartment without noticing they'd been there.

So I went outside and walked up the street to meet my distant relatives. Near the closed shop of Uri the Romanian shoemaker, I saw them getting off the bus. The man was very tall, wide and heavy. The upper button of his coat was fastened tight below his chin. His wife was small and frail, her head reaching his hip. While they walked down the street toward me, his hand was resting open and heavy on her head.

I won't write about this hand and won't tell about it. I continued watching them as they came closer, and wondered what was there to write about a hand anyhow.

While I was sitting with my visitors around the table at home, my wife serving refreshments, my relative's hand brought another hand to mind: that of Yaakov the wagon driver, my neighbor from Kiryat Tivon. He used to tell me that in Poland he always turned oxen upside-down for slaughter with his own bare hands. He suspected I didn't believe him and suggested I shake hands with him. He'd press lightly, and any whiff of doubt I might have would blow away.

"Come on, stick your five in mine," he said.

He repeated it every time we met. At times I nearly gave in, but as soon as I saw his hand I held back.

"No," I said.

Ten years as good neighbors I never gave in.

I did give in when he was dying.

They called from Kiryat Tivon for me to come and say goodbye. When I stood by his bed, there was no longer anything to see but his teeth. The man had shrunk and crumpled into a small bundle. He opened his eyes and asked to shake my hand. I didn't hold back. Why should I be afraid of a man on his deathbed? When the dying man shook my outstretched hand, any doubt I had was blown away.

I've never told this story or put it down in writing. But now, with the two hands in contact with one another, that of my relative's resting on his wife's head and that of the dying wagon driver's pressing mine, the pressure was strong.

Nevertheless, I told myself, I'd hold back. Between one sip and another my relative was listing his problems and those of the State. While nodding at his words, I succeeded taking my mind off the two hands. But now I remembered the giant wagon driver who turned into a small bundle.

A similar thing happened once to an ox in Kibbutz Givat. Early in the morning on my way to the sheep shed, I saw it filling up the whole cowshed with its presence. In the evening on my way back from the field, there was nothing left where it was slaughtered but its skin — a small folded bundle.

Two bundles now filled my head, that of the wagon driver and that of the ox, along with two hands, that of the wagon driver and that of my relative.

With all this in my mind I accompanied my relatives back to the bus. We walked up Zangvil Street and stopped at the shoemaker's shop, already open after the midday break. Uri the shoemaker answered my greetings. He unfolded and spread out the sheet of leather he was holding, checked the goods and asked himself if a decent pair of shoes could come out of it.

When the bus arrived and my visitors left, I couldn't hold back anymore. On my way back home down Zangvil Street, I spread out my relative's hand resting on his wife's head, the dying wagon driver's hand shaking mine, and the two bundles, that of the ox and that of the wagon driver, and asked myself in Uri the Shoemaker's voice if a good story could come out of it.

Notes on the Stories

Blood Connection

1. Yochanan Zaid. Son of Alexander Zaid (1886-July 10, 1938), a founder of the Jewish defense organizations Bar Giora and Hashomer, and a prominent figure of the Second Aliyah.

2. Hashomer Ha-Ivri. Hebrew Defender/Guard organization

3. While so many suffered in Ukraine, the Ungarin consider Kiev to be more holy than Jerusalem. They are, however, unable to return to their place of origin. They do not recognize Jerusalem/Israel and only will when the Messiah comes.

A Wet Man by the Traffic Light

1. Mount of Rest at Herzl Boulevard. Israel's military and national cemetery; also called Har HaZikaron, or Mount of Remembrance. Named for Theodore Herzl, founder of political Zionism, whose tomb is here.

The Crumb Picker

1. HaPalmach. A street in the Katamon neighborhood named for the

elite fighting force of the Haganah, the underground army of the Jewish community during the time of the British Mandate for Palestine.

2. Ze'ev Jabotinsky (1880-1940). Zionist leader, also a poet and novelist, founder of the Jewish Self-Defense Organization in Odessa and co-founder of the Jewish Legion of the British army during WWI. He was a leader in forming Jewish fighting groups during the Mandate.

3. Islamic Museum. Located on the Temple Mountain, adjacent to the al-Aqsa Mosque.

The Love Dance

1. "desecration of ancient bones." A common occurrence for the ultra-religious is to protest almost every new building or road, claiming the land to be an ancient cemetery.

Something Good in This Country

1. "didn't make tzimmes over." A Yiddish expression, meaning "to make a big fuss over" something. Tzimmes is actually a sweet dish typically made of carrots, dried fruits and other root vegetables.

2. "Homage to Jerusalem Stabile," a well-known sculpture prominently displayed in Jerusalem's Holland Square, is one of the last by Alexander Calder.

Customer on the Way

1. *Alteh Zachn.* Literally, "old things," in Yiddish. Worn, secondhand

— actually tenthhand! It's a derogatory phrase. When used in context of buying and selling, it represents the lowest kind of merchandise.

2. Kohen. Priestly class of Jews. See glossary: Kohen, Levite, Israelite.

3. Ezekiel. Biblical prophet, mostly known for his Resurrection prophecy. The shop owner's name is Ezekiel Yish-Tamim, literally, The Righteous One. It is also the epithet used in the Bible to describe Noah (Yossel Birstein's father's name was Noah).

Reflections

1. See Psalm 121:1, an expression of confidence in God's care and protection: "I turn my eyes to the mountains; / From whence will my help come?"

The Man from the Bus

1. Blood libel. Falacious anti-Semitic accusation that Jews kidnapped and murdered Christian children as part of religious rituals.

2. See Psalm 114:4. "Mountains skipped like rams, hills like young sheep."

The Broom

1. Jaffa Gate. One of eight stone portals in the walls of the Old City of Jerusalem.

2. The Via Dolorosa. Way of Grief. A street in Jerusalem, where Jesus

is believed to have walked carrying the cross on the way to his crucifixion.

The Substitute

1. Jerusalem Day. An Israeli holiday commemorating the reunification of Jerusalem and the establishment of Israeli control over the Old City.

2. See Psalm 121:1.

Glossary

Aliyah. In Hebrew, the "ascent." Its meaning, the immigration of Jews, the "going up" to the Land of Israel.

Chasid (variant of Hasid; pl. Chasidim). Sect of Orthodox Judaism that promotes spirituality and faith through mysticism, prayer, and joy; founded in Poland in the 18th century by the Baal Shem Tov (Master of the Good Name) in reaction to legalistic Judaism. Today there are numerous Chasidic dynasties, among them, Chabad Lubavitch, Satmar, and Ger.

Hittites. Second of the twelve Canaanite nations, listed in the Book of Genesis. Descended from Ham, son of Noah.

Hittlemacher. Yiddish, for hatmaker.

Jebusites. Identified among the Canaanites. By some, identical with the Hittites. Questionable whether they inhabited Jerusalem until defeated by King David.

Kaddish. The traditional Jewish prayer that a mourner recites.

Kapota. Black gown worn by many ultra-Orthodox Jewish men.

Kohen, Levite, Israelite. Ancient division of Jews during the Temple periods (c. 9th century BCE — 70 CE): Kohens, the priestly class, performed ritual services and animal sacrifices; Levites supported the Kohens in their duties; Israelites were of the lay class.

Mahaneh Yehuda Market. Often referred to as The Shuk — a popular, bustling marketplace with more than 250 vendors and many juice bars, cafés, and restaurants.

Mea Shearim. Among the oldest Jewish neighborhoods in Jerusalem — largely populated by strictly Orthodox Jews.

Minyan. A quorum of ten Jewish men required for a prayer service.

Mount of Rest (Har HaMenuchot). Also known as *Givat Shaul,* the largest cemetery in Jerusalem.

Perizzites. According to the Bible, this tribe dwelled in the south of Canaan. "The Israelites settled among the Canaanites, Hittites, Amorites, Perizzites, Hivites, and Jebusites" (Judges 3:5).

Second Aliyah. Refers to the immigration of some 20,000 Jews to Palestine, mostly from the Russian Empire, 1904-1914.

Selichot. Penitential prayers recited on days before Rosh Hashanah, the Jewish New Year.

Shabbat Square. Well-known central location in Jerusalem.

Shiva. In Judaism, the traditional mourning period for the dead. It begins immediately after a funeral and lasts for seven days.

Shtetl. Small Jewish town or village in Eastern Europe before World War II.

Shtreimel. Fur hats worn by married, ultra-Orthodox Jewish men, and in some Jerusalem communities, generally only after marriage and, in some neighborhoods, by boys who have been bar mitzvahed.

Tallit katan. A fringed prayer garment traditionally worn by men, either under or over one's clothing.

Ultra-Orthodox. Strictly Orthodox, or Haredi, Jews who reject modern secular culture. Haredi derives from the Hebrew word for fear, *harada*, and has been interpreted as "one who trembles in awe of God" (Isaiah 66:2,5).

Ungarin (lit. Hungarian) neighborhood. An ultra-Orthodox neighborhood in Jerusalem.

Wailing Wall, or Western Wall. Remnant of the ancient wall surrounding the Second Temple, destroyed by the Romans in 70 CE.

Yarmulke, also called a kipa. A round cap worn mostly by Orthodox and Conservative Jewish men, especially during prayer.

Yeshiva. Jewish education institution that focuses on the study of religious texts, primarily the Talmud and Torah.

A Comma's Tale: On the Translation

Jorge Luis Borges once told his translator not to write what he said but what he meant to say. And in these translated bus stories what Yossel Birstein meant to say is brought out best by how the story is told. At the base of Yossel's distinctive telling are the Yiddish inflections he grew up with that were then influenced by his years of English in Australia, followed by an immersion in Hebrew after he and his wife Margaret made Aliyah.

In reworking Margaret Birstein's original translations of Yossel's stories, Hana and I read the original Hebrew over and over. Off the page, they became more alive and so a great deal of our effort went into working over how these stories were voiced. Towards this end, our more difficult challenges had to do with pacing and rhythm — in translating Yossel's voice into English, we were especially sensitive to punctuation.

It wasn't until working on "About Patches and Bears" that we both realized we were trying to convey Yossel's "gut language," how he told his stories, and how we heard them. Consider the following sentences (italicized words are for illustration):

> But her dream for a kiss went hand in hand with her anxiety over the shabby dress. She'd run and hide away as soon as he'd appear at the low entrance to the backyard. From her *place on the worn bench she noticed that even small people had to bend down when entering the yard, and in the market Simon was the tallest of them all.* He'd have to bend very low, and she'd have time to hide away in the yard.

In ordinary English, a comma would follow "From her place on the worn bench"; and in early drafts we had one, though the Hebrew does not. The comma signifies a slight pause — it clarifies the beginning of the sentence, giving the reader a moment to absorb the girl's perspective. However, we ended up removing the comma for that reason: with it, the bench is more of a resting place, a physical location. That wasn't the story's implication though: "her place on the worn bench" also indicates a state of mind.

"The Fifth Smile" provides another example of how

hearing the stories in Yossel's voice is not merely a matter of accurately translating the literal Hebrew sentence. In speaking of Rudolph, a blind man the narrator once took care of, Yossel writes, "He had a youthful voice, and his laughter was also youthful." In early drafts, we had considered paring down this sentence to delete what seemed like unnecessary repetition with, for instance, "He had a youthful voice and laughter." However, we realized this pared version was a poor translation of a story that is strongly visual. We ended up aligning the English with the Hebrew. In our translation, both the comma with its pause and repetition makes laughter more of a separate character.

The punctuation, especially commas, rather than being a pause because of grammar is a pause because of context. It is a storyteller's pause — one of either meaning or music or both. Yossel's voice, rather than the literal Hebrew or grammar, influenced our choices on punctuation. As a result we have sentences where our use of punctuation is sometimes incorrect in standard English grammar.

Many types of sentences like the following in "The Broom" occur throughout *And So Is the Bus*: "Nowadays he was a neighbor of mine in Jerusalem, and joined the ride at the last moment." Though the comma in this sentence is incorrect, its use here indicates that joining the ride is separate from being a neighbor — rather, joining the ride is a direct consequence of being the speaker's neighbor. This pause also implies the slight, emotional distance between the speaker and neighbor, as is apparent from the rest of the story. We tried a number of alternatives, for instance, " … and he joined … " instead of just "joined." In this alternative, however, the comma's pause balanced the first part of the sentence with the last. This balance implies being a neighbor is just as important as "joining the ride," which is not what the story and voice convey.

The effects of punctuation in each story are seemingly small. However, taken together, from story to story, they add up. They help modulate the pacing and rhythm of Yossel's sentences that are central to the wit and empathy in his voice informing each story.

Robert Manaster
Champaign, Illinois

Biographies

Yossel Birstein
Translators and Contributors

Yossel Birstein, 1920-2003

Yossel Birstein was born in Biala Podlask, a small Polish town about 100 miles east of Warsaw. Like most Polish-born Jewish children, he studied in a cheder, a private Jewish school that taught the fundamentals of Judaism. In 1936, at age 16, he immigrated to Australia to join his grandparents, who were already living there. On the ship, he met the painter Yosl Bergner, also 16. The two of them became life-long friends. Apart from one sister who also made her way to Australia, Yossel's parents and two siblings were killed during the Holocaust.

In 1941, Yossel married Margaret Weisberg, then went on to serve four years in the Australian Army during WWII. The couple had a daughter, Hana, in Australia. After the war he edited a Yiddish-English periodical for Jewish youth at the Kadimah Jewish Center in Melbourne. In 1950, Yossel, his wife, and baby daughter Hana made Aliyah and settled in Kibbutz Gevat in northern Israel, where he worked as a shepherd for the next eleven years. A second daughter,

Nurit, was born on the kibbutz. In a radio interview Yossel explained how he began as a shepherd:

> When I came to Gevat I was welcomed by a man called Haim Gevati, who later on became the Minister of Agriculture. Already then, as the Kibbutz manager, Mr. Gevati had a long-term agricultural view. He said to me, "Yossel, you came from Australia, the land of sheep? Here's a herd and you will be its shepherd." In truth, throughout the 14 years I'd lived in Melbourne I hadn't seen even a tail of a sheep. At any rate, I became a shepherd."

In 1961, Yossel and his family moved to Kiryat Tivon, a town some ten miles south of Haifa. He began working as a clerk in Bank Ha'Poalim and soon became an expert in stock-exchange investments. This job became the background of his book *The Beneficiaries*. In 1975, Yossel resigned from the bank and moved with his wife Margaret to Natzeret Illit (Upper Nazareth), where he dedicated his time solely to writing. In 1982, the couple moved to Jerusalem where Margaret is still living.

* * *

Yossel began his literary career by writing poems in Yiddish; they were collected in *Under Alien Skies*, published in Melbourne in 1949, and included Yosl Bergner's drawings. From then on, Yossel wrote only prose. In 1958, his first novel, *On Narrow Sidewalks*, was published in Yiddish and a year later in Hebrew; this novel was the first Yiddish book to describe life in the kibbutz. Yossel wrote most of his books in Yiddish, which he translated into Hebrew with the help of Nissim Aloni and Menakhem Perry.

He also translated many literary works from Yiddish to Hebrew and from Hebrew to Yiddish. When Yossel and Margaret moved to Jerusalem, he also began working in the Hebrew University's National Library, where he handled the archive of Yiddish poet Melech Ravitch. This job gave rise to *A Face in the Clouds*. In 1995, Yossel's last novel *Do Not Call Me Job* came out. It tells the story of people who wander between Poland, Australia, and Israel.

A few years after Yossel and his wife moved to Jerusalem, he was asked to write a weekly story about Jerusalem for the periodical *The City's Voice*. In 2000, his best Jerusalem stories were collected in *Stories Dancing in the Streets of Jerusalem*. Most of tthe stories in *And So Is the Bus* are taken from this last collection; two more stories have been added from *Stories from the Realm of Tranquility*, a book published posthumously. Yossel died on December 23, 2003, at age 83.

Tel Aviv University professor, critic, and publisher Menakhem Perry, Yossel's publisher and editor, wrote of him, "I consider Yossel Birstein one of the three-four-five greatest Jewish authors of the 20th century, and I'm talking about the scale of Kafka and Agnon."

Although *And So Is the Bus* is the first collection of Yossel Birstein's work in English, his writing has been translated into a number of other languages. His books have won the Itzik Manger Award for Yiddish Literature as well as the Prime Minister Award for Hebrew writers.

Translators and Contributors

MARGARET BIRSTEIN was born in Frankfurt, Germany in 1924. She was 12 when her family managed to escape Hitler's regime and immigrate to Melbourne, Australia. There she met Yossel and the two married in 1941. Margaret gave birth to their first daughter, Hana, in 1947; three years later the small family made Aliyah. They settled in Kibbutz Gevat, where Nurit, their second daughter, was born in 1956, and Margaret began her career as an English teacher. She continued teaching high school English when she and Yossel moved to Kiryat Tivon, then to Upper Nazareth, and eventually to Jerusalem.

Margaret had always been Yossel's first and most valuable audience. It was on her that he always tried out his stories. For many years she was the translator of all his books and stories. Now retired, Margaret lives in Jerusalem. She is a grandmother of six and a great-grandmother of eight.

* * *

HANA INBAR is the older daughter of Yossel and Margaret Birstein. Born in Melbourne, Australia, she was three when the family arrived in Israel. Except for the years 2000 to 2013 when she worked in high technnology jobs in the U.S., she has lived in Israel. She chose high-tech as her profession, though maintained her "inherited" interest in literature. Living in Champaign, Illinois, she met her co-translator, Robert Manaster. They began a joint project by translating Israeli poet Ronny Someck's work into English.

Hana is now living in Kefar Sava in Israel with her second husband, the photographer Benjamin Lapid. Between them Hana and Benny have five children and ten grandchildren. In retirement, she dedicates much of her time to studying the untranslatable meanings of the Bible that underlie the Hebrew text.

* * *

ROBERT MANASTER is a poet and translator. His poems have appeared in many journals including Rosebud, Image, International Poetry Review, The Literary Review and Spillway. Robert and Hana's translation of Ronny Someck's The Milk Underground (White Pine Press, 2015) has been awarded the Cliff Becker Book Prize in Translation. Robert has also been awarded several Illinois Arts Council grants as well as residencies at Ragdale, the Midwest Writing Center and elsewhere. He lives in Champaign, Illinois.

* * *

NURIT SHANY was born in 1956 in Kibbutz Gvat. She started painting at age four and was encouraged and trained by her father's best friend, Yosl Bergner. She was five when her family left the Kibbutz for a family home in Kiryat Tivon — Hana's most vivid memory of Nurit is that she couldn't keep her hands off any blank surface that came her way. She drew and painted on their bedroom walls, on her bed linen, on her own legs, arms, and belly, as well as on every single one of her school notebooks. Nurit graduated from the Bezalel Academy of Art in Jerusalem. Her paintings are being exhibited at some of the more prestigious art galleries in Tel Aviv.

During the last decade of Yossel's life, Nurit accompanied him on his numerous storytelling tours; she also became a superb storyteller. After Yossel's death, Nurit established a children's theater where she performed as an actress. For many years she lived in Tzur-Hadassah, a small town near

Jerusalem, where she and her then-husband Ehud Shany raised their two daughters, Tout and Gili. In 2010 Nurit moved to Tel Aviv and opened an independent studio where she is "living and painting happily ever after."

* * *

CLIVE SINCLAIR is the author of fourteen books, and the winner of three literary awards: the Somerset Maugham, the Jewish Quarterly, and the PEN Silver Pen. In 1983 he was one of the original Best of Young British Novelists. He holds a doctorate from the University of East Anglia for his work on Israel Joshua and Isaac Bashevis Singer. He lives in London with the painter Haidee Becker, and a hound called Lobos.

AND SO IS THE BUS
BY YOSSEL BIRSTEIN
is designed by Sandy Rodgers. The text is typeset
in Fournier Standard and the titles in Fournier
Standard Italic; the book is printed on acid-free papers
by McNaughton & Gunn, Saline, Michigan.